MW01222953

Dopemage

S.F. Lydon

Copyright

No portion of this book may be reproduced or distributed in any form without permission from the Publisher

Names, characters, products, etc. are used from the author's imagination, as this is a work of fiction. If there is any resemblance to any establishment or person living or dead, it is purely coincidental

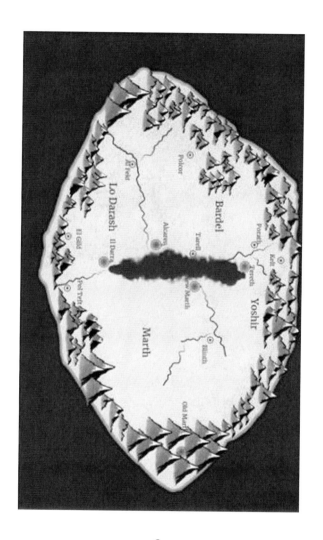

Table of Contents

Prologue

It was a cloudy night in the Heights, the richest district in Alcaren. Boran and Bisil, the twin moons, shed nearly no light through the cloudy sky; the Ninestars' bluish light was dim in the north. The grounds around Lord Aster's manor were dark except for the torches held by the various guards that patrolled them. Lissa sat perched on the outer wall of the manor estate, the last of her cannin cigarette burning down. She was dressed in tight, black clothing, her dark hair pulled into a braid and tucked down the back of her shirt.

As she waited for the right time to make her move, she couldn't help but examine the pristine manor house and meticulously manicured grounds. It was galling how the people of the Heights lived in such extravagance while the people of the slums lived hand to mouth under the thumb of various gangs. Lissa would like to think that her mission tonight was about getting back at them, but the reality was that she was being paid very well for what she was about to do.

The manor itself was dark, a good sign that her intel was correct; Lord Aster was not here. Likely he was attending some fancy gathering hosted by one of the other rich snobs who lived here. The guard patrols were moving toward each other now, probably to pass on status reports on the rest of the manor grounds. This would be her best chance.

Lissa pulled a tin of baccin from her jacket pocket and removed the lid. The ground leaves looked like thick, moist dirt, and as much as she disliked using this form of the drug, she couldn't risk smoking it and the smell attracting someone's attention. She took a pinch of the baccin and stuffed it into her bottom lip.

The effect was profound as she drew on the power provided by the substance. All her senses increased. She could see the individual faces of each guard in their flickering torchlight. She could hear their muttered conversation. She could feel the bumps and grooves of the stone wall she was crouched upon. Everything was sharp and clear, even in the gloomy night.

Lissa grabbed the ledge beneath her and swung down, her fingers finding holds in what would appear to be a smooth wall. Her feet pressed firmly against the wall for support, she began to climb down the thirty-foot façade. She dropped the last ten feet and slipped behind a tree.

She observed the two groups of guards, knowing they would separate and head in opposite directions any minute. Sure enough, after another few exchanges, the guards turned away from each other. One group headed for the front of the manor, the other headed toward the back. Lissa slipped around the tree and headed for the manor. As she got closer, she drew upon the cannin in her body and pushed her mind outward.

It was a strange experience, even for a person of Lissa's experience. She could feel the individual minds of the guards in each group, even though they were now almost fifty yards away on each side. She kept her touch feather-light, gently pushing a command into each of their minds.

Ignore the west side of the manor. No one is there.

The command would last for a while; Lissa was a talented Fogger and had used a substantial amount of cannin. It was a tricky thing, to properly

Fog someone without pushing so hard that they noticed something was wrong.

Lissa reached the wall of the manor and surveyed the climb she would need to make. Statues lined the vast expanse of stone at five-foot intervals, each one at least seven feet tall. Balconies were aplenty along the second and third story. That was the thing about these rich types; their inclination towards ostentation left plenty of options for a thief to use.

Lissa approached one of the statues, a tall, well-built man of stone with a large axe extended upwards. It was clearly a depiction of one of the Nalathi, the servants of the Nine Creators who had remained to guide humanity after the Nine's betrayal. She wasn't sure which one it was meant to be. Torguntr or Aracles, who had braved the Three Hells, perhaps. She was not particularly religious.

Lissa swung herself up onto the statue, climbing up to stand upon the outstretched arm. The baccin gave her an unusually keen sense of balance. She then leaped up to the second-floor balcony above her. Her fingers just managed to snag the edge of the overhang. She pulled herself up and slipped over the railing.

According to the maid she had bribed, the balcony on the third floor to her right would get her into the room she needed. Lissa judged the distance; it would be a difficult leap. It would be easy enough if she had some coccin, but it was unwise to mix too many substances at once; she was already using baccin and cannin.

Lissa balanced herself on the railing of the balcony she was on, then decided on another strategy. She stepped back down, walking back to the far edge of the balcony. It was about eight feet across; it should be just enough to give her the momentum she would need. She set herself, then set off at a quick sprint, leaping up at the last moment. She planted her right foot on the railing and threw herself up toward the target balcony.

Lissa's aim was slightly off, and she found herself both too high and too low. She was too high to catch the bottom ledge but too low to reach the top of the railing. The best she could do was allow herself to hit the ledge with her middle and throw her arms around the railing supports. The blow knocked the wind out of her, but she managed to hold on.

After a minute, Lissa was able to pull herself up and slide over the railing. She took a moment to regain her composure before turning toward the balcony doors. The room beyond was dark, but her enhanced vision let her see the well-tidied study inside. She pulled a small knife from her boot and used it to slip the simple latch on the doors.

Lissa found herself shaking her head at the lack of real security measures these kinds of people paid attention to. They thought that because they could afford guards that they wouldn't need quality locks.

Once inside, she headed to the desk to the right. Lissa reached under the desktop and ran her fingers over the smooth wood until she found the spot she knew would be there. Again, her information came from the maid she had paid off.

It was a small square of raised wood that would have been noticeable even without her baccin-enhanced senses. Lissa pressed it in, hearing the faint click. A small drawer popped out of the other side of the desk.

Lissa stepped around to the front of the desk and pulled the small drawer open. Inside were three bags of cloth. The first two she opened had coins, all golden thrones, the highest denomination of currency. It was a small fortune.

The last bag had the real treasure, however. It was filled with a soft brown powder. This was what she was after. She slipped it into her jacket pocket with a small smile.

The wagon rolled along the cobblestone streets of Alcaren, wheels creaking, carriage bouncing through the night. Aside from the driver, the wagon had a single occupant. Harlon "Halfjaw" Gage sat among stacks of boxes in the bed of the wagon. He had long, lank black hair and a scraggly attempt at a beard that did little to hide the deformed jaw beneath. His dark eyes were half-lidded, almost on the verge of sleep. The pipe sticking from the corner of his mouth was tilted almost to the point of slipping out, baccin smoke drifting from the bowl.

Gage hated these late-night guard jobs. He did not see why they could not wait until the morning to transport these wares from the ship up to the Heights. Especially since they needed to cross such a large section of the worst parts of the city to get there from the docks. He did not know what was in the crates that filled the wagon, but he knew he did not care. Some things couldn't be helped. Plus, he was paid very well not to care what was in them so long as they reached their destination. Alcaren's position on the Sliver Sea made it an optimal trade port. There could be goods from anywhere on Kalkis in those boxes.

Gage took an unconscious puff of the pipe, the sting of the baccus leaf filling his throat and lungs. The usual sting struck hardest in the ruined part of his jaw, a section with no teeth, just raw gums. He always took care to keep a little baccin in his system to keep his senses sharp on these assignments.

There was very little light in this part of the city. Streetlamps were few and far between, and if one happened to go out before dawn, it was sure to stay that way. The cobbles were uneven around here and potholes were common. All that combined with the chill night air of autumn, made for a dark, uncomfortable ride. But Gage had endured worse and had no problem resting his tired eyes despite the less-than-ideal conditions. An attack was unlikely in any event. His employer was known for his attention to security, and the sigil of his shipping company was plain on both sides of the wagon.

Even as these thoughts rolled through Gage's head, the wagon began to slow, the two horses neighing in response to the pull of the reins. It was far too early to have reached the gates that separated the Heights from the slums.

"Gage." The driver's voice cut through the night air. Gage looked up at the tension in the man's voice. He had known the driver, a man called Faron, for a few years now. They had worked a number of times together, often for this same employer. Faron's hand was reaching back into the wagon toward the loaded flatbow he kept there.

Gage placed his pipe on the seat next to him and stood up in the bed of the wagon, looking up the street at the five men holding clubs who stood barring their way. His hand slipped into his coat pocket and palmed the small glass vial he kept there. A sound behind him alerted him. He looked over his shoulder and saw two more men step into the street behind the wagon, each armed like the others.

"Take the two behind," Gage said to Faron while calmly pulling the stopper of the vial. He tapped some of the chalk-white powder onto the back of his hand and snorted it with a deliberate tilt of his head. If the would-be bandits were smart, they would notice the sign of a Rager preparing for a fight and seek better pickings elsewhere. "I'll take the ones in front."

Gage shivered as the drug coursed through him. It had been a good long time since he had used coccin, and the feeling was as exquisite as ever. He could feel the power thrumming in his veins, waiting for him to draw upon it.

The strangers advanced on the wagon, apparently undeterred by Gage's mild theatrics. He leapt down from the wagon as time slowed around him. He rushed at the men, moving faster than they could hope to match. He reached the first before the man knew he was there and grabbed him by the neck. The immense strength granted him by the coccin allowed him to hurl the man across the street like a doll. He chopped at the neck of a second man and threw his knee into the stomach of a third. Each of the targets were tossed to the ground like sacks of meal.

But something was not right. Gage should have felt their bones break beneath his strikes. Blood should be flooding the cobbles and misting the air. He was about to turn on the fourth man when he noticed the first man starting to rise from where he had crashed. Faron's cry cut through the haze of his coccin fueled bloodlust.

"Lurchers!"

Gage looked around, trying to determine which of the bandits Faron was referring to. As he did, he saw the other two men he had struck were also getting up. On the far side of the wagon, a flatbow bolt lay on the ground directly in front of one of the bandits; it clearly had struck him with no effect.

Gage looked at each bandit in turn and realized his error. They each had somewhat dazed looks, and the slumped, stumbling posture of a drunkard.

They were all Lurchers.

16

Two of them closed in on Gage swinging their cudgels with the wild abandon of a man with no ability to aim. The blows missed by a wide margin. None of the Lurchers could hope to match Gage's speed or strength so long as the coccin lasted, but he would be unable to harm them so long as they had alcohol left in their system. But he would be damned if he did not try. He lunged forward, ducking one blow, and sunk his fist into the belly of one of the Lurchers. The blow lifted him off his feet and hurled him back toward the wagon. He hit the cobblestones with what should have been a bone-crushing impact but was almost immediately getting back to his feet.

The man that Gage had struck first was leaning against the side of a building, his arm hanging slightly askew. That was good, it meant he was losing his imperviousness. Gage struck a few more blows, each one flinging a Lurcher across the street, but none having any real effect. By the time Gage looked again, the first man had pulled a flask from his jacket pocket and downed the contents; undoubtedly more liquor. He looked at Gage with a leery, slack-jawed sort of grin.

Before he could think of a new strategy, the other Lurchers were back on him. He ducked and dodged their blows, returning each with a swift, powerful strike of his own. But each time they got right back up and stumbled back into the fray.

Gage soon realized that all seven were now around him, swinging their cudgels with no coordination or control, even occasionally hitting each other. But the cudgels had even less effect than his own attacks. He tried to get a glimpse of Faron but could not see through the crowd of attackers. He began to feel his high lessening. If he ran out of coccin before he managed to incapacitate his opponents or drive them off, he would be bludgeoned to death in seconds.

"The wagon!" One of the Lurchers yelled at the others. Two of them backed off and shuffled toward the wagon, turning the horses around, while the others continued their assault on Gage. He was really slowing down now. He had some coccin left in his vial, but he would never get a spare moment to use it.

Finally, one of his blows paid off. His fist took one of the men in the chest and staved it in like a barrel of thin wood. The man collapsed, his struggling lungs making a wet, raspy sound briefly before stopping.

"Back!" The lead Lurcher yelled. "Get the wagon out and pull back!"

The Lurchers scrambled drunkenly for the wagon, climbing or in some cases simply heaving themselves over the sides, as it began to roll away. Gage was almost completely sober now. He took the vial out again as the wagon pulled away down the street. He tapped out the last of the coccin powder and snorted it. It was not enough to last long, but it might be enough to take a few more thieves.

Gage began to sprint as the drugs filled him with energy again. The wagon was almost a hundred yards away, but he knew he could catch it. He took virtually no notice of Faron's limp, bloody body lying on the cobbles as he flew past. The buildings blurred around him as he sped down the street. The wagon drawing closer and closer with each second.

Fifty yards away.

Then twenty.

Now ten.

Gage heaved himself through the air. He felt the coccin running out as he soared through the air, closing on the back of the wagon. He realized at the exact last instant that he was going to be short by about a foot. Just before he missed entirely, he threw both arms forward, punching down on the back edge of the bed. His fists shattered the backboards and tossed several of the crates into the air.

Gage struck the street with a bone-jarring crunch. The breath was crushed out of him and his hands stung where the wood had cut him. He rolled onto his back, gasping for air like a landed fish, as the crates he had knocked from the back of the wagon crashed onto the cobbles around him.

Gage's last thought as he fought to keep from passing out was that, for the first time in his life, he had failed.

Dane awoke in darkness. His hands were secured above his head with thick, hempen rope. He was sitting against a dirt wall; his legs splayed out before him. His head pounded and his mouth was dry. Nausea hit him like a blow as soon as he opened his eyes. It was too dark to make out where he was, but it dawned on him as his memory came back.

It started when his friends, Fram and Peg had dared him to steal some of his father's whisky. Dane hadn't really wanted to do it, but at fifteen his friends had decided they were old enough to try alcohol. After all, they were old enough to work the fields like men, why shouldn't they get to drink like men?

So, Dane had done it. While his father was at the market, selling some of their recent harvest, Dane had taken a bottle of Penluck Rye from his father's whisky cellar. They had gone out to the barn and drank almost the whole bottle before they were found. Fram was passed out at that point and Peg wasn't far behind. Dane had been too drunk to stand but was still conscious when his father walked in.

To say that his father, Farlen, had been angry was an understatement. He had harshly woken Fram and Peg from their stupors and sent them stumbling home. Then he had turned his attention on Dane. Farlen had always been a stern father. He was prone to cuffs and cruel words. But what followed this indiscretion was nothing short of attempted murder. Except that each blow he landed on Dane seemed to have no effect.

The beating should have killed Dane, or at least maimed him for life. Instead, each strike felt like the passing of the wind; they touched Dane but had no impact. It took a few minutes for Farlen to see through his rage and realize none of his blows were having any effect.

Dane could still see the moment his father realized what he was. The shock, the revulsion, then the greed. He could see that Farlen quickly processed the opportunity he had.

His son was a dopemage.

In the cities, there were options for dopemages. They could join the city watch, or the army. Or they could sell their services to criminals or independent merchants. But in the country, it only went one way. Any dopemage found in the rural areas was almost always sold to the army by their family.

When Farlen realized what he had, he had taken a staff and beat Dane until the alcohol wore off. When the blows began to cause damage, Farlen had beaten Dane senseless.

And now, here he was. Dane was tied up in what he could guess was the very whisky cellar he had stolen from.

The sound of the cellar door being pulled open caused Dane to jerk his head toward where he knew the stairs would be. The light of a lantern lit the steps as a figure descended.

Dane began to panic. How long had he been unconscious? Had his father already fetched an officer to take him in? As the figure reached the bottom of the stairs, Dane could see it was Farlen. Was he here to drag Dane to the army outpost himself?

Farlen approached Dane, his hard, weathered face inscrutable in the lantern light. The light ignited a new level of pain in his already throbbing head.

"Good, you're awake." Farlen inspected Dane's bonds. Apparently satisfied, he stepped back. "I always thought you were useless, but apparently, I was wrong." Farlen stared down at Dane, something in his face was different. Dane had always known his father resented the fact that his mother had died giving birth to him. But this was something different. There was an open loathing on his father's face. For the first time, Dane realized that his father hated him.

"W-what are you going to do with me?" Dane wished he could keep the quaver out of his voice but it was impossible.

"What do you think?" Farlen leered at Dane; it was the closest thing Dane had ever seen to a smile on his father's face. "I'm gonna turn you in, boy. The army's always lookin' for new dopemages. You'll finally be worth somethin' to me." The leer faded from his face and Farlen regarded Dane again with his typical disdain. "I'll be a couple hours to the outpost and back. Then I'll be rid of you and a damn sight richer for it." Farlen spat at Dane's feet and turned, heading back to the cellar stairs.

Dane wanted to call out, to beg his father to reconsider. But he didn't. Some part of him had already decided that a life in the army, even a life where he would be used as a weapon until he died, was preferable to this miserable existence with Farlen.

Farlen left him in total darkness again. Dane let his head fall back against the rough dirt wall, hoping he could at least get a few hours of sleep before his new life began. He was drifting off, when he heard the sound of the cellar door being opened.

Dane straightened up as much as he could. His father couldn't possibly have found the outpost and returned in the short time he had dozed.

A figure descended the cellar steps, but there was no torchlight. Instead, the figure held a shining crystal in his right hand. He reached the bottom of the steps and held the crystal aloft, shining light across the cellar. He stopped when he noticed Dane.

The man approached Dane. He was middle-aged, average height and slender build. His hair and beard were the same shade of iron-grey and cut to the same length, creating a bristly frame for his face. His eyes were dark, almost black.   He approached Dane, regarding him as a man might regard a horse he was considering buying.

"Tell me," the man said, "if you had the choice, would you serve in the army, or would you forge your own path?"

Dane wasn't sure what to say. He had not had the time to consider what he would do if he had options. It had never occurred to him that he might ever have options.

"Who are you?" The stranger smirked. "I am someone who believes in freedom." He looked at Dane with those dark eyes, as if he could see right through him. "So, again I ask, would you forge your own path?"

"Yes," Dane answered. The response came from his mouth almost before the thought even entered his mind. However, he found that it was true.

"Good," the stranger said. He pulled a knife from his cloak. Dane flinched as the man approached, but all he did was cut the ropes holding his hands bound to the wall.

Dane stared at his free hands in disbelief. He looked up at the stranger, unable to process what was happening.

"Here, take these," the stranger tossed two things into Dane's lap. One was a metal flask. The other was a small bag of coins. "Go to Alcaren. You can make something of yourself with your abilities there." He smirked again. "Perhaps I'll meet you there someday." With that, the stranger turned and strode away. He was at the top of the cellar steps before Dane even managed to get the loosened ropes off his wrists.

Dane didn't know what to make of the interaction. He couldn't believe he was suddenly free. But one thing he did know. He would not wait around for his father to return. He was resolved of one thing. He was going to go to Alcaren. He would forge his destiny.

Chapter 1

Lissa walked down the street, her boots clicking on the cobblestones. She wore tight breeches tucked into the boots, a white shirt that buttoned in the front. Her blue jacket hugged her figure until it reached her waist, where it flared out the sides and back. Her midnight black hair was pulled back in a braid that hung almost to the small of her back.

The noon sun shone down, showing the main street of Hollows for the near-rundown mess it was. The buildings were made of old wood, paint peeling and shingles missing. Hollows was one of the larger slums of Alcaren. It was controlled by a gang known as the Fangs. They were led by a man named Marcum Grant, Lissa's boss.

Hollows was relatively nice compared to other slums, like Tricks or the Mill. Each slum tended to specialize in certain forms of trade. Hollows was known for its cannin dens. Cannin wasn't legal, strictly speaking, but the king didn't care much about what went on in the slums and Grant paid the city watch an ample number of bribes to turn their heads. Other substances, such as coccin or poprin, were much more firmly controlled. But cannin was seen as relatively harmless.

Lissa felt the urge to turn into one of the several cannin dens that lined this street, she'd always enjoyed smoking the stuff, even if it didn't give her power. She resisted the pull of it and continued on to her destination. She reached the Smokey Pipe, a large tavern that, unlike the other buildings on the street, was built of stone.

Lissa entered the tavern and nodded to the barman. He was a lanky man, balding with beady brown eyes. Miles was his name, and he was one of Grant's top men. He often posed as a barman to avoid suspicion. Miles nodded toward the back and went back to polishing a glass.

Lissa walked to the back of the room and through a door that opened into a hallway. The hallway had no other doors but the one at the end. In front of that door stood an enormously fat man. He had dark Darashi skin like Lissa and a shaved head. He stood at least six and a half feet tall and must have weighed at least thirty stone.

"Dosk," Lissa said, nodding her head toward the door behind him. "He ready for me?"

Arman Dosk was Grant's most capable bodyguard and one of the most talented dopemages in the city. Because of his size, most people would assume he was a Lurcher. But Lissa knew he was an incredibly dangerous Rager, a dopemage who specialized in coccin use. She saw little point to a bodyguard so deep in their own territory, but apparently a rumor from several years back of someone who wanted to take Grant down had unsettled him. The habit had stuck even though nothing had come of the rumor.

"He's got someone in there now, but could be he'd want you in too," Dosk held up a hand for Lissa to wait and knocked on the door three times. A muffled voice sounded from within and Dosk nodded to Lissa before opening the door for her.

The room was large and richly appointed. Several plush-looking chairs were set around a fireplace at one end of the room. A bar stocked with expensive liquors and wines ran along one wall. At the other end of the room two fancily carved wooden chairs sat facing a massive desk. The desk was made of intricately carved

30

mahogany, designs and figures crawled across its surface.

Marcum Grant sat behind the desk. He was a portly man in his middle years. His short dark hair was peppered with grey, and his face was clean-shaven. His green eyes shone with intelligence, though they were set deep in his round face. His nose was lined with broken veins and his cheeks were red, the only visible signs of his rampant alcoholism.

Grant was not a dopemage, nor was he a strong warrior. But he was devious. Most of the other gangs were led by a hierarchy of dopemages, the strongest on top. But Grant had found a better way. Rather than simply let the strongest lead and decide who got what, he had started the Fangs with the idea that the smartest should lead, and spoils should be earned individually. This idea had grown into one of the three strongest gangs in the city. And it was the main reason he took his personal security so seriously. Unlike most other gang leaders, he had no magic to protect him if someone tried to kill him...and many had tried.

A man sat in one of the chairs facing the desk. He sat forward, his long dark hair falling around his face. It wasn't until she reached the desk that she saw who it was.

Harlon Gage.

Everyone called him "Halfjaw" now, on account of the disfigured side of his face. A white scar ran from near his ear down to his jawline, through the black hairs of his scraggly beard. Worse, the corner of his jaw looked as if it had been pushed inward, as if someone had carved the jawbone out. No one knew how he had sustained the injury that caused it, but the result was an uneven face that caused most men to grimace.

His grey eyes found her blue ones; recognition flashed in them. Lissa was glad of that; it hadn't been so long since she had last seen him that he should have forgotten her. His black coat was slung over the back of the chair, so he was sitting in just his shirt with the sleeves rolled up. His hands and forearms were covered in scrapes and cuts. His trousers were torn and muddied as well. Lissa had been his apprentice for a while, but she wasn't sure what he had been up to recently; it didn't look like it had gone well for him. She knew very little of what he had been up to after her apprenticeship with him ended. All she really knew was that he had taken another after her, but it hadn't lasted long.

"Sir," Lissa said, addressing Grant. She nodded to Halfjaw and he nodded back, then turned his attention to Grant.

"Ah, Lissa!" Grant welcomed her. "I trust your mission last night went well?"

"It did, sir." Grant smiled at that, though he did no more than that, indicating that they would speak of it later.

"Good, good." He gestured to Haljaw. "I'm sure you remember our guest. It hasn't been that long since he left us for greener pastures. Eh, Gage?" Even Grant was wise enough to not call him Halfjaw to his face.

Some men might have taken the reference to his leaving their gang for private employment as a barb, but Halfjaw just stared at Grant, as if waiting for an answer.

"Of course, sir." Lissa wanted to ask why he was here now but knew better than to rush things. Grant was a bit of a showman; he liked to do things in his own way.

"Well, it seems our friend here is in a bit of a pickle," Grant smiled widely at that. It wasn't often that someone like Halfjaw needed a favor. "Apparently, he was robbed last night. He is eager to see his master's goods recovered as quickly as possible."

Lissa was stunned. Someone had not only tried to rob Halfjaw, but they had succeeded. The whole reason Halfjaw had been able to leave their gang was because he was widely regarded as the most dangerous man in the city. He was one of the few men the city watch knew for sure was a dopemage but didn't dare try to arrest.

Not that being a dopemage was illegal, exactly, unlike in Lissa's home city of Il Darra. No, it wasn't illegal, but anyone with access to the magic was obligated by law to turn themselves in for service in the military.

But no one dared to try pressing Halfjaw.

Lissa looked at the disfigured man, he met her eyes but kept silent.

"Who would dare to steal from him?" Lissa looked back at Grant. He still looked like he was barely keeping from laughing.

"Unfortunately, that is why he is here." Grant turned his smug look back on Halfjaw. "He was unable to identify the thieves during the attack. So, he came to me to see if I could help him. I have yet to hear anything about an attack like he described but then, this was never my area of expertise." Grant looked at Lissa. "So, I offered your help in this matter. You have some experience tracking thieves as well as many useful contacts throughout the slums. I'm sure you will prove invaluable to Gage in recovering his goods." Lissa was surprised by that. Grant rarely lent out any of his agents to outside jobs.

"They aren't my goods," Halfjaw spoke for the first time. "They belong to my employer." It was the first time Lissa had heard him speak since his injury. He had always been gruff and quiet, but his voice now had a slurring quality to it. The words sounded like they were being forced out through clenched teeth.

"Of course, of course!" Grant replied with an oily smile. Lissa was surprised by how much pleasure he took in Halfjaw's predicament. Grant was a clever man, and he could be ruthless at times, but he had never seemed cruel to her before. Perhaps Halfjaw's departure for private employment had been more offensive to Grant than she had noticed before. "So, Lissa? I assume you have no problem helping out our old friend?"

That was a ridiculous question. Grant was her boss, if he gave her a job, she did it. Simple as that. "No problem at all, sir." She turned back to Halfjaw. "What information do you have on the thieves?"

"They attacked us on the Dockside avenue, just inside the edge of Blinders territory," Halfjaw began, "Seven men, all Lurchers. Killed my driver and took the carriage. I killed one, busted up the back of the wagon. Managed to recover a few of the boxes." It wasn't much to go on.

"The one you killed, what did he look like?" Lissa would need something to give her contacts, some piece of information to look for.

"Typical Lurcher; slow, big. Brown hair, brown eyes. No identifying marks." Lissa nodded. This would not be easy.

"Alright, I'll spread the word to my people. See what comes up but I probably won't have word until tomorrow at the earliest." Halfjaw nodded

36

and rose to leave, grabbing his jacket off the back of the chair.

"We can meet here. Tomorrow night." With that, he left, walking with a slight limp.

Grant got up with a sigh. He made his way over to the bar and poured himself a glass of whiskey. He offered the bottle to her, but she shook her head. She had never taken to alcohol, despite the benefits for a dopemage.

"Are we expecting a reward for this job, sir?" Lissa didn't know what Halfjaw's employer dealt in, but it was likely very valuable.

"I should think so," Grant said with a snort, before throwing back the glass of whiskey. "But honestly? It was almost worth a bag of gold just to see Ol' Halfjaw sitting here, asking for help." He laughed at that. He poured another glass then returned to his seat. "Now, the matter of your mission?" He held out his hand.

Lissa pulled the small bag of brown powder from the inner pocket of her jacket and handed it over. Grant held it up, smiling at it.

It was poprin, the rarest and most strictly controlled narcotic in the world. Undoubtedly, Grant would make a fortune selling the stuff one spoonful at a time. He reached into his desk and pulled out a cloth bag. He tossed it to her.

Lissa caught the bag, hearing the coins clink inside. She didn't need to count it, Grant was very good at paying his people. She knew it would hold the full thirty gold marks she was owed for the job.

Grant set the bag of poprin down on his desk. "I have another errand I need you to run. Nothing difficult, you'll be able to manage it while you help Halfjaw with his investigation." He looked up at her, his green eyes looking unusually eager. "Krayden has a new toy that I'm interested in testing out. I've already arranged for it to be paid for, just need you to pick it up for me."

"Of course, sir."

Grant waved his hand toward the door. "Better get started, Halfjaw didn't give you much to go on. Good luck." He chuckled again, likely still giddy about Halfjaw's predicament. Lissa turned and left the room. It was true that Halfjaw hadn't given her much, but she had the best informants of anyone in the gang. One source in particular that no one would ever think of.

Chapter 2

Gage's mood was sour as he left the Pipe. Not only had he been robbed the night before, but he had been forced to come here and ask Grant for help. He'd had to sit across from him and suffer the smug attitude of that grasping drunkard. Gage had never liked Grant, despite working for him for almost a decade. The man fancied himself a genius but in reality, he was just another thug who had found a clever way of never having to do the real work himself.

At least he had agreed to help. It would be nice to work with Lissa again. She was competent and resourceful. More of a thief than a fighter, but she could hold her own in a pinch. And most importantly, she never let the drugs rule her.

The biggest problem with working with dopemages was that too many of them didn't treat the substances they used with the proper respect and fear. They saw them first as a means of gaining power, and second as a means of pleasure. That had been one of the biggest motivations for Gage agreeing to work for a private employer.

Unfortunately, his years away from the streets had meant that when he had tried to investigate the robbery, most of his previous contacts were no longer around. The ones that were had succumbed to their addictions to the point of uselessness.

He made his way to Arches, the slum closest to the Heights. It was considered a slum since it sat outside the walls of the inner city, but it was the slum where anyone with any real money lived. It was far nicer than the rest of the slums, and the city watch was far more active here. It was the only slum not controlled by one of the various gangs.

Gage lived in an apartment on the third floor of a nice stone building. His unit was at the back corner of the building, his instincts for self-preservation leading him to pick the most defensible and secure one he could find. It had three rooms, not counting the privy: a main room with a small kitchen, a bedroom, and an office.

Gage entered the office and went straight to the closet. He opened it and shifted aside the clutter he had piled upon the three boxes he had recovered from the street where the robbery had occurred. He took the first one over to the simple wooden desk in the corner and set it down. He hadn't looked too closely at the contents of the boxes yet, but from a cursory inspection, they appeared to be documents regarding trade expeditions.

If he couldn't chase down the thieves on the street, then he would have to try finding some clue as to who might have wanted the information being transported. Could it have been a rival merchant hiring a gang of random thugs? Or a nobleman with a grudge who had used his hirelings disguised as street rats?

As he sifted through the papers, these thoughts burning in his mind, his tongue probed at the right side of his mouth. It was a habit he had developed ever since his disfigurement. His tongue ran along the strange configuration of muscle and ligament that connected the remnants of his jaw to his skull. The area was sensitive, as always. Every motion of his face hurt. Chewing, talking, even swallowing a mouthful of water, were very painful.

But some things couldn't be helped.

The alternative was something Gage refused to let himself consider. What he had done had been necessary. He didn't like to think about that day. The pain of the knife. The cracking and pulling of his jawbone. The brown powder and the euphoria that had followed.

No, it was best not to think of that.

A knock on the front door of his apartment jolted him out of his reverie. Gage quickly tucked the boxes away in the closet and went to answer the door. He pulled it open to reveal a tall, thin man. He was pale, with a large nose and a shaved head. Gage recognized him immediately. His name was Torol Stane and he served as a go-between for Gage and his employer.

Behind him stood two bodyguards. One was even taller than Torol and heavily muscled. That was Boram. He had been a member of a gang called the Wreckers. They were a notoriously brutal group, though not particularly successful. The other was short and unremarkable looking. Brown hair and brown eyes with a typical build, he was not an impressive man. However, Gage knew him. His name was Rello, a well-known Rager. He was a man who enjoyed fighting more than most.

"Gage," Torol said as he walked into the apartment. "I'm sure you know why I'm here." He looked at Gage as if he were something to be scraped off a boot. Gage had never liked Torol. There were several reasons, but this one, the attitude that he was so much better than Gage just because he had the luck to be born on the right side of the wall. It didn't help that their mutual employer had an enormous amount of influence in the city, so much that Torol felt himself an extension of that influence rather than the tool he was.

"The robbery?" It wasn't a question, but Gage had never been good at showing proper respect to people who thought they were better than him.

"Yes," Torol looked around the main room with distaste. "I assume you are working on finding the people responsible and inflicting a fitting punishment for them?" His tone implied that he was disappointed that Gage had not managed it already, despite it being less than a day since the incident. "Frankly, I think our employer will be very surprised when he hears of this. This is the sort of thing you were hired to prevent.

Perhaps I shall have to discuss with him a change in personnel."

Although Torol said it in a voice that sounded almost bored, Gage could see the smile in his eyes. He was happy to have something to criticize.

"I am." Gage said it in his usual monotone. He could have addressed the rest of what Torol had said, but Gage was smart enough to just let it roll off his back. It would annoy the man that couldn't fluster Gage, plus he wasn't interested into getting in an argument. It wasn't worth the pain.

"Is that all you have to say for your failure?" The smile was gone from Torol's eyes. Gage's response had done more than annoy him. He could see the fury in the tall man's face. "Let me make this clear." He stepped forward so that he looked straight down at Gage. It was a move meant to intimidate, but Gage had never really understood it. Gage had never been tall or imposing, something that led to people often trying this very thing. Until they found out what Gage could do. Being taller didn't make you better, stronger, or more talented. It just meant you had further to fall when you got knocked down.

"You will recover the stolen goods and administer an appropriate retaliation in one week, or I can guarantee your employment will reach an abrupt conclusion!" Boram cracked his knuckles, an obvious sign to Gage exactly what that conclusion would be like. He glanced at the two thugs. Boram's posturing didn't faze him, but there was something in Rello's expression, an emptiness, that he found unnerving. That one was definitely the more dangerous of the two.

Gage wanted nothing more than to strike Torol at that moment. It would be so easy, and so satisfying to see the smug prick hit the floor. But then he'd have to fight the other two and he was less sure about how that fight would go than when he had first seen them. So instead, he simply nodded.

Torol gave him a look of disgust mixed with anger that he wouldn't answer verbally. As if Gage were some savage just because he was stingy with words. Torol wouldn't be so eager and eloquent if his words cost him the same pain they did Gage. Torol turned up his nose and strode from the apartment in a way he probably thought looked imperious.

Gage watched him go, unimpressed. In a fair world, men like Torol would get what they deserved someday. They would see how wrong they were and realize they were fools. But the world wasn't fair. And some things couldn't be helped.

Chapter 3

The night was overcast, with very little light from the moons reaching through and no stars visible except the Nine. Dane was hoping the cloudy night wouldn't turn to rain before he found some place to sleep. He wandered through the streets, keeping to the shadows, wary of anyone he saw. There weren't many people about, but the taverns and dope dens were lit, and the noise of rowdy customers spilled from their doors each time they opened. Very few streetlamps were glowing in this section of the slums; he wasn't sure which one he was in anymore.

Dane had reached Alcaren two days before and within a couple hours he had been robbed and beaten twice. The first time had been for the money he had gotten from the stranger. The second was for his coat and his boots. He had no alcohol so he could not fuel his powers, plus he wasn't confident he knew enough about them to use them effectively, even if he did.

His socks had torn through in several places, so his bare feet were bruised and scraped by now. Still, he stumbled along, searching for some little alley or abandoned shack he might be able to shelter in. The climate in this part of the world was warm year-round, so while the nights could get chilly, the cold would not kill him.

His first night in the city he had slept in an alley, huddled up against the back of a bakery. The owner had found him at first light and chased him off, warning him not to come back. The second night he had found an old warehouse that was half collapsed. It had seemed a decent place to spend the night. Unfortunately, he wasn't the only one who thought so. Dane had been awakened midway through the night to a group of grimy young men kicking him awake and threatening him with clubs.

Since then, Dane had just been wandering around, doing his best to avoid being noticed. His only food had been scraps he had picked out of a dumpster. After a day and a half without a drink, he had finally given in and lapped some water from a puddle in the street. He was beginning to think he would be better off turning himself in to the constables as a dopemage and joining the military.

It occurred to Dane, not for the first time, what a ridiculous idea it had been to come here. The stranger had given him no information on how to use his powers or anyone to contact to find work. He felt like a complete fool.

As he passed another small alley, he noticed the distinct glow of firelight. Dane paused and leaned against the mouth of the alley. It extended about thirty feet before dead ending in a high wooden wall. Two figures sat side by side in front of a metal bin. The fire was set in the bin, burning an assortment of garbage, judging by the smell. Unlike most of the people Dane had seen, they were not glancing around suspiciously, watching for someone who might try to steal what comfort they had. Nor were they stuffing their faces with whatever they had found to eat or engaging in one form of substance abuse or another. They sat comfortably and seemed unaware of the dangerous city around them.

This made Dane nervous. Anyone who could sit comfortably in this city must be dangerous. And yet, there was something pulling at Dane's mind, an unspoken invitation. He longed for the warmth of the fire, even if it would do nothing for his hunger or thirst. He was about halfway down the alley when his fear got the better of him. He was about to turn and run when one of the figures spoke.

"You alright there, lad?" He lifted his head and Dane could see his features in the dancing light of the fire. His face was lined with wrinkles and his features were thin. He had a head of grey hair that fell in a matted mess down his back, and a ragged grey beard flowed down to his chest. His shoulders looked thin and bony under the blanket he had wrapped around his body.

In contrast, his companion was a massive man. Even sitting, he was almost as tall as Dane, standing and built like a Marthen bull. He must have been nearly seven feet tall when fully upright. He sat hunched f-orward, completely still. The firelight played over his skin which was dark, like a Darathi. His face and head were completely clean shaven, and his lips appeared to be moving, though no sound came out. Both men sat on wooden crates turned upside down.

Dane froze where he stood, feeling like he should run, but there was something in the man's voice that kept him from doing so. It took him a moment to realize what it was.

Kindness. It felt like it had been a very long time since anyone had spoken to him with kindness in their voice.

"Looking for a place to rest a bit?" The man asked. "Plenty of room to spare 'round the fire." He waved his hand toward the spot across the fire. The man had a strange accent that Dane couldn't place. He'd heard traders from Lo Darath, Yoshir, and even New Marth, but he had never heard anyone like this man.

"Might even have some drink to spare." That caught Dane's attention. If he could get some alcohol, he could at least prevent himself from being hurt again.

Dane approached the fire slowly and sat on the ground. The warmth of the fire was a welcome change from the chilly night air. Up close, he could see that the big man was indeed muttering to himself, although he could not make out what the man was saying. He also noticed that each man wore a ring. The big man wore a ring of what looked like black stone on his left hand and the hairy man wore a similar one of white stone on his right.

"Here lad," the hairy man tossed him a battered silver flask, "have a drink. You look like you could use it." Dane twisted the top off and took a small sip. The liquor burned in his throat, and he almost spat it out. It was far harder than anything he had ever tried before.

"Never had grain alcohol before, lad?" The hairy man chuckled softly. "It's harsh stuff, but it's easy to get down here. It's what the Narcomancers use."

"Narcomancers?" Dane had never heard that word before.

"Ah, right. You probably call them dopemages down here." The hairy man took the flask back from Dane and took a swig. "Narcomancer is a fancy term. It's what the educated folk call them." Dane nodded. This was good information to have. It might be easier to find a job as a dopemage if he could appear more knowledgeable about the subject.

"You got a name, lad?" The man leaned forward, inspecting Dane with wide, green eyes.

"Dane."

"Well, Dane. I'm Hal," the hairy man patted his chest, "and this is Gun." He slapped the big man on the shoulder as he said the name. Gun did not respond to the introduction, just continued to sit there muttering to himself.

Dane could feel the alcohol warming him and allowing his body to relax. His head was pleasantly light, and his thoughts felt less depressive. He also felt something else. An energy that ran through his veins, presenting itself like a new sense, waiting to be used. He had not noticed this sensation when he drank the stolen whiskey, but then he hadn't known he was a dopemage.

The looseness brought on by the alcohol gave him the courage to speak more. "What's wrong with him?" He nodded to Gun. "Is he mad?"

"Mad?" Hal stroked his filthy, tangled beard. "No, mad doesn't quite capture it. Incurably insane is closer to the mark." He said it without judgment or malice. It was simply a fact. Dane wasn't sure how to take the news. People with afflictions like that were said to be unpredictable and dangerous. But Gun didn't seem dangerous, despite his size. He seemed broken and pitiable.

"How long have you been in the city?" Hal asked. "You have the look of someone new to this place. A bit out of your depth, eh?" Dane felt his cheeks redden in embarrassment. Back on his father's farm, he had considered himself rather resourceful. But here, he had quickly realized that he had overestimated himself.

"Out of my depth?" Dane replied. "That doesn't quite capture it. I fear 'drowning' is closer to the mark." For a brief moment, Dane felt a spike of anxiety at his cheeky reply. His tongue had often gotten him in trouble with his father.

But Hal simply laughed at the quip. "Oh, clever boy, clever!" Dane relaxed at that. It felt nice for someone to laugh at his attempts at humor rather than ignoring them, or worse, lashing out because they didn't appreciate them.

"Well lad —" Hal cut off. His gaze went beyond Dane toward the mouth of the alley. Dane spun around leaping to his feet. Three men stood there, two held clubs while one had a long knife. Hal groaned and muttered to himself before forcing himself to his feet as the men started toward them.

"Hello, gentlemen!" Hal addressed them with no fear, although there was a touch of weariness in his voice. "There is plenty of warmth to share, if you would be so kind as to put down those weapons. Friends shouldn't need to go armed around friends." The men paused about ten feet away.

"We ain't your friends, old man." The man holding the knife stepped closer and the firelight illuminated his thin face. His dark eyes were close set, and his nose was long and almost as sharp as the blade he carried. "Give over everything you have and find a new spot. This one's ours now."

Hal sighed. "Must it be this way?" He seemed to be growing wearier by the second.

"'fraid it does. But if yer easy about it, we won't kill you. Best offer."

"So, my turn comes again," Hal said with a shake of his head. Dane had backed against the side wall of the alley by now. He could feel the power in his veins, boosted by fear, begging to be used. But Dane's terror kept him from moving.

Hal bent down next to Gun as the men with the clubs advanced. He touched the white ring on his hand to the black one on Gun's. The white stone ring glowed with light, and the light *flowed* from Hal's ring to Gun's, leaving Hal's ring black.

Dane watched with horrified fascination as Hal immediately collapsed to the ground. He began to shake and sob, his green eyes wide with terror at some unseen horror. Gun, however, lifted his head, his brown eyes clear, his muttering had stopped.

The first of the two men with clubs rounded the fire coming at Gun with his weapon held high. Gun stood up and caught the man's wrist before he could bring the club down. Gun twisted the man's arm to the side; the snap of the man's bones was audible even to Dane on the other side of the alley. The man's screams of pain were cut off quickly as Gun struck the man in the throat. He collapsed to the ground gasping for breath that wouldn't come.

Dane watched, stunned, as the second man swung his club in a two-handed blow at Gun's back. Gun twisted out of the way with impossible speed and struck the man on the side of the head as he stumbled past. The man fell limply to cobbles. Gun stood tall and there seemed to be a red mist rising from his skin. His eyes met Dane's, then widened in surprise.

Dane turned his head just in time to see the man with the knife bearing down on him. The man had obviously decided on pursuing weaker prey while Gun was dealing with the other two. He thrust his knife forward at Dane's chest, and in the moment before it struck, Dane felt something instinctual within himself activate. The knife struck his chest, pushing him back against the wall. Before the man could even pull back from the thrust, Gun had him in a chokehold from behind. Gun flexed his massive arms and twisted, snapping the man's neck, and dropping him to the ground.

Dane felt his hold on the alcohol fueled energy slip and he slid to the ground, the sudden loss of power leaving him unsteady. Gun dropped to his knees before Dane, running his hands over Dane's chest and abdomen. He pulled back suddenly, realizing there was no wound.

"You are a Narcomancer." Gun's voice was deep, and his accent differed from Hal's but equally strange. Dane nodded, finding it hard to speak. He understood very little of what had just happened. Hal had done something with those rings. Something unnatural.

Thinking suddenly of Hal drew Dane's attention back to the dirty man who still huddled on the ground, tears streaming from his sightless eyes. Gun walked over to him, a look of pity in his eyes. He bent down and touched his ring to Hal's. The same odd transfer of light happened, leaving Gun's ring black and Hal's white. Gun immediately sat back onto his crate, his head drooping, and his muttering resumed. Hal sat up slowly, wiping his face on his sleeve.

He stood and looked around, surveying the scene. His eyes finally found Dane's.

"So, lad. You're a dopemage." It was not a question. Dane was suddenly afraid. These men were dangerous and unnatural, even if they had been kind to him. He could do nothing other than nod, though the action made his vision spin.

"Well, suppose you better keep this then." Hal tossed the battered flask back to Dane. It landed in his lap, his hands too slow to catch it. "Come on, lad. We had best be gone from here, quick. Someone is bound to notice three dead men and even down here that's not something to be ignored."

Hal grabbed a sack from behind the crate he had been sitting on, reached down to take Gun's arm, and pulled him to his feet. He led the big man, who followed placidly toward the street, not bothering to extinguish the fire. Dane could think of nothing else to do, so he pushed himself up, tucked the flask into his pocket, and followed the two madmen.

Chapter 4

Lissa stepped out of her apartment building to the morning sun's blinding light. It was a beautiful morning, though it did nothing to ease her frustration. She had spent the last two days searching for information about the robbery, but so far, had found nothing. She had asked every mole she could find about rumors or hints. No one had any helpful information for her.

Lissa had one more potential source but so far, she hadn't been able to find him. He hadn't been in any of his usual haunts, but it was worth the effort to keep looking. Hal always knew more than he should about the city's goings on. Even if he was a lunatic.

She headed toward Tricks, one of the few slums she had not checked yet. Primarily because of her deep aversion for the place. It was filled with brothels and other, less official means of prostitution. It was a painful picture of what her own life could have become if her powers hadn't manifested. She thought it unlikely that Hal would be there, but he had a habit of being in unlikely places.

Lissa barely managed to get more than a couple blocks when a large crowd around the mouth of an alley drew her attention. She stepped up to the back of the crowd, trying to peer through at whatever scene had drawn them. All she could see were a couple men wearing the black and gold uniform of the constabulary.

"What happened here?" Lissa asked a tall, thin man beside her who had a much better view over the crowd.

"Triple murder last night," the man answered. "Looks like some kinda giant was at them. Bodies all broken and tossed around."

Lissa immediately thought of the big man, Gun, that Hal always had with him. She had never heard the man speak or even seen him move, but he looked strong enough to inflict wounds such as the man described. She tried to think of where they might have gone after fleeing the scene. Unfortunately, it was difficult to predict the ways of a madman.

Lissa decided to start at the place least likely to be searched for a murderer. She headed for Arches, keeping an open eye on each alley she passed. She lit a cigarette as she walked, using the baccin to enhance her eyesight, intent on not missing them. She was almost at the border of Arches when she caught a glimpse out of the corner of her eye. Three figures sat under the eaves of a squat, run-down tavern. One was massive and still, another thin with an untamed thatch of beard and hair wrapped in an old blanket.

The third one puzzled her. It was a thin figure curled up asleep on the filthy cobbles. Its back was to her, so she could see nothing else of who it might be. The other two were clearly Hal and Gun, though she had never known them to have another person join them.

Hal looked up as she approached them. "Ah, pretty Lissa!" Hal always seemed happy to see her. "What brings you to visit us on this fine morning?" The thin figure on the ground stirred; she could now see it was a young boy.

"I need some information, Hal." Lissa looked down again at the boy who was rubbing

63

sleep from his eyes. "You finally made another friend, huh?" Hal chuckled at that.

"Information, eh? Well, I know lots of things. Like the Alephi hillmen were the first to see all ten worlds. Or, that the Spire of the Sun, built by the Druadan is the tallest structure ever built? Before it sank into the sea, anyway." Hal grinned at her as if this information was impressive rather than pure nonsense. "As for the boy, he just happened to fall in with us last night."

"That reminds me, Hal. Was that your handiwork I saw this morning? The constables are actually interested in it."

"My handiwork? Dear no!" Hal shook his head, tangled beard swaying. "That was all Gun here." He patted the big man's shoulder. "But don't worry, they won't get a confession out of him!" She didn't doubt it.

"Well either way, better lay low for a while." Hal just smiled at her. He really was insane. "What made you take the boy in?" The boy was now awake and was staring at her.

"Well, as it happens, I was hoping to introduce him to you." Hal leaned forward as if to share some secret. "He's a *Narcomancer!*" Lissa's eyes widened in surprise. New dopemages in the city were rare as the bounty for turning them in to the military usually persuaded people to rat. "You're sure, Hal?" Lissa was imagining the possibilities now. If she brought Grant a new unaffiliated dopemage, she would likely get a bonus. Plus, another dopemage in the gang would lighten the load of grunt work she had to do and allow her to focus on her specialty burglary jobs.

"Sure am! Saw it with my own eyes. Well, Gun's eyes actually, but I trust them." Lissa looked back at the boy.

"Is it true?" The boy looked down at the ground. "Kid, I can help you, but only if you're honest with me. If you're taking advantage of these loonies to try to scam me, it won't go well for you. But if you really are a dopemage, I can get you a job, shelter, and see you trained in your gifts." The boy looked back up at her, then nodded slowly. "Alright then, you can come with me when I'm done here." She turned back to Hal. "I need to know anything you might know about a robbery of a merchant's wagon that happened three nights ago."

"Ah, you mean your friend Halfjaw letting those Lurchers get the better of him." Hal grinned bigger than before, showing a few missing teeth. "I've heard little enough about it myself. But I believe a man named Bull might know more. Ask around, you should be able to locate him easy enough." Just like the other times Lissa had asked Hal these kinds of questions, a gold mist seemed to rise from his skin as he spoke. It dissipated quickly, making her doubt if it had been there at all.

"Well, thanks for the tip, Hal. I'll take the stray off your hands now and leave you to do…whatever it is you do all day."

"Mighty kind of you pretty Lissa. We do happen to be quite busy."

Lissa doubted that very much. She waved for the boy to follow him and turned back the way she had come. She paused when she didn't feel him following. She turned back to see him facing Hal.

"Thank you for your help, Hal." The boy held out his hand, which Hal shook gently. "I just have to ask…"

"Go ahead, lad. Ask it." Hal seemed to know what he was thinking.

"Well, *what are you*?"

Hal's face was somber as he responded. "We're just a couple old men, wanting to be forgotten." He patted the boy on his shoulder. "Go on, lad. Your time with us is over for now."

The boy nodded and turned to follow Lissa.

"What's your name, boy?"

"Dane." The reply came in a quiet voice. She could only imagine what a time he had on the streets before finding his way to Hal. She wouldn't typically have called that "luck," but in this case, it turned out to be. "Can you tell —" She cut him off with a sharp motion of her hand.

"We don't discuss our business out in the open. We can talk when we get somewhere more private."

They walked in silence all the way back to Hollows. She led him to the Pipe, walking straight in and turning toward a table in the far corner, away from where anyone might overhear them. They sat on opposite sides of the table, and she looked him over intently. Dane was average height, but clearly still growing. His hair was light brown and slightly curly. There was a light dusting of light brown hairs on his chin and upper lip. Unremarkable looking, which could be a great asset as a Narcomancer.

"How long have you known about your abilities?" Lissa asked.

"Only a few days. My dad was going to give me to the military, so I ran away." Dane looked down at the tabletop, avoiding her eyes. He was timid, but she was much the same when she started out. His confidence would grow with his abilities.

"How did you find out?"

"Got really drunk with some friends. My dad found me and started beating on me. Noticed that it wasn't hurting like it should." Lissa nodded at that. It was a typical tale.

"Have you tried anything other than Lurching?" Dane shook his head. That was good. Some dopemages weren't discovered before they began experimenting. This often led to them having a hard time learning to be disciplined about using.

"Why is it called 'Lurching?'"

"It's just a reference to the sloppy, stumbling way that drunks tend to move." Dane nodded at that; it was an easy concept to grasp.

"Do you have any booze on you now?"

Dane nodded, pulling a battered flask from his pocket.

"Take a drink." Dane did, sipping from the flask. He grimaced as the liquor hit his mouth. "No, no, kid. A real drink. You'll need to learn to stomach this stuff sooner or later. Might as well start now." Dane closed his eyes and took a longer pull. His cheeks bulged as he struggled to keep it down. "You good? Not gonna puke right? Cuz if you puke, you'll lose a lot of the effect." After a pause, Dane nodded that he was okay. "Do you feel the power in you? Can you draw on it?" Dane nodded again and opened his eyes.

Then, Lissa punched him in the face.

The blow knocked the boy from his chair to the floor. He lay there stunned. Lissa got up and walked around the table. She took the boy's face in her hands and examined it. There wasn't even a hint of a mark.

"Sorry about that," Lissa said, "just had to be sure you were telling the truth."

Dane lay there, at a loss for words until Lissa reached down and pulled him up by the arm. "Come on, time to meet your new boss."

Lissa led him to the back hall and toward Grant's office. Dosk was in his customary place by the door.

"Got a surprise for the boss. Is he available?" Dosk eyed Dane as he knocked twice on the door. Grant's voice came through the door, bidding them to enter. Lissa grabbed Dane's arm again and towed him into the office.

Grant sat behind his desk, rifling through a stack of papers. A cigar was in his mouth and a glass of whiskey sat on the desktop.

"Lissa! Have you brought that item I asked you to pick up from Krayden's? And who is your friend?" He puffed on his cigar and eyed Dane as appraisingly as a jeweler might a suspect gem.

"Actually, sir, I haven't been to Krayden's yet. I have been preoccupied with my other errand. However, during my investigation, I came across this young man. His name is Dane, and he is a Narcomancer. More importantly, he is new to the city and unaffiliated." Lissa could not keep pride out of her voice.

"Oho! That is big news!" Grant smiled broadly now. "Have you explained what we do and what inclusion in our association would entail to him?"

"Not yet, sir. I figured you would want to do that yourself." Grant always wanted to initiate new dopemages himself.

"Right you are, girl, right you are." Grant motioned for Dane to step forward and the boy complied. "Tell me son, what brings you to our fair city?" Dane explained again how he had discovered his abilities and what had caused him to come to Alcaren.

"Interesting. Very interesting." Grant let out a large puff of smoke. "Do you understand what we do here? That the things we engage in are often, shall we say, extralegal?"

"Yes, sir." The boy looked both nervous but resolved.

"Good, good. Now, a lot will be asked of you here. But unlike the military, the manner in which you use your powers and the kinds of jobs you do will be left up to you, for the most part. While they may not fall within the exact parameters of the law, you will be well compensated. In addition, you will have the support and protection of our organization. Does that sound fair to you?"

Dane nodded without hesitation. Grant nodded back and extended his hand across the desk. Dane reached out and shook it.

"Lissa will see to your training and will find you a place to stay until you earn enough to arrange your own lodgings." Grant turned his attention back to Lissa. "This presents an excellent opportunity. You can take him to Krayden's with you and introduce him to Tally while you pick up my package." Lissa could hear the slight reprimand in his tone that said he had expected her to get the package already. It was slight, but it was there.

"I quite agree, sir. I'll have it for you tonight." Grant nodded. Lissa took Dane by the arm and steered him toward the door.

"Come on, kid. You got a lot to learn, and I'm a busy woman."

Chapter 5

Gage watched the messenger run off down the street before turning and walking the other way. The message was from Lissa, telling him to meet her at Krayden's. Apparently, she had found some sort of lead. Krayden's wasn't far, just on the other side of Arches.

He walked down the street, lost in thought. He had found no leads and the clock was winding down on his deadline. Four more days. Gage wasn't sure what exactly Torol had in mind as a punishment for failing but it was better to focus on not failing than what might happen if he did. Besides, there were other things on his mind.

It had been three full days since he had last taken a snort of coccin. There was an itch in the back of his mind, urging him to take a pinch and shove it up his nose or even just wipe it on his gums. But he wouldn't give in. Discipline was the key to lasting as a Narcomancer.

Gage lit the plain, brown pipe he had found to replace his lost white hartshorn one. Inhaling the puff of baccin helped to alleviate the itch for coccin. There was a burning sting to the baccin smoke. He had never liked it and once had greatly preferred the baccin chew. He missed the burning in his lip as it settled in. But he wouldn't dare to chew anymore. He would not tempt fate that way again.

These thoughts and urges were the price for the power of Narcomancy. It was a high price, but one that he, like many others, paid willingly. Some things couldn't be helped.

Gage arrived at Krayden's and saw no sign of Lissa, so he leaned his back against the rough stone wall of the two-story building and waited. Krayden was well known as the best producer of narcotics in all the slums, maybe in all the city. Well known among the gangs anyway, he was a simple apothecary to anyone on the right side of the law. He was also paid handsomely by Grant to keep tabs on all the Narcomancers in the city.

It didn't take long for Lissa to appear. She had a boy with her, gangly with brown hair and brown eyes.

"Who's the kid?' Gage grunted as Lissa reached him.

"New apprentice." Lissa pulled open the door to the shop without another word. Gage followed her in, the boy following behind him. Krayden sat behind the counter that ran across the middle of the front room. He was a thin, older man with white hair that was receding and a neatly trimmed beard. He wore a pair of small, delicate-looking spectacles that rested on his large nose.

"Lady Lissa! I have been expecting you." The old man moved around the end of the counter. He was dressed in an older fashion; a short jacket over a white shirt, pants that fell over his boots and held up by suspenders. "I have Mr. Grant's order ready. Shall I fetch it?"

"Not just yet, Krayden," Lissa smiled at him. "I have someone who needs to meet Tally." She waved her hand at the boy. "This is Dane. He's a new member of our organization and is inexperienced with his abilities."

"Mmm, found another one, have you?" Krayden reached over to the counter and rang a small silver bell.

"It wasn't exactly me who found him but yes. He needs to learn the basics and Tally is the best for that sort of thing."

"That she is, that she is." As he spoke a door to the back of the shop opened and a short, sturdy looking woman walked through. She was dressed in a floor length green skirt and a white shirt with a black vest over it. Typical garb for a merchant or tradeswoman.

"Oh, well now isn't this a party!" Tally spoke in a high, excited voice. "Miss Lissa! So nice to see you again! And Master Gage! Looking grim as always! And who do we have here?" She practically pranced around them, stopping in front of the boy.

"Dane, ma'am." The boy said in a quiet voice.

"Oh, so shy, this one! And none of that ma'am business! It's just Tally from now on young master Dane." She turned from him and walked back toward Gage, getting far closer than he generally was comfortable with. "Now Master Gage, it's been a good long time since I've seen you! Lost a piece of your face since then! I hear they call you Halfjaw now, but it's not so bad as all that! You can't be missing more than a quarter of it at least!"

Gage was trying to think of something to say to that. No one had dared to call him "Halfjaw" to his face since soon after his disfigurement. He had quickly earned a reputation for intolerance toward the moniker. But before he could do or say anything impulsive, Lissa stepped in.

"Well, 'Three-Quarter Jaw' just doesn't roll off the tongue." She gave Krayden a pointed look. Gage was glad she was here to take charge. He wasn't a clever-tongued man and his impulse to solve problems violently had only grown with time, but he kept himself reined in and settled for glaring down at Tally with his stone-grey eyes.

Krayden noticed Lissa's glance and cleared his throat. "Right, hmm, well Tally, dear. Young Dane here needs an introduction into the arts of Narcomancy. I'm sure he would do well with your assistance."

"Of course! Well then Dane, come with me! We'll need to go down to the basement to get started." Tally grabbed Dane by the arm and towed him towards the back room. Dane looked at Lissa over his shoulder, but she just nodded at him to go ahead.

Once they had passed through and the door had swung shut, Lissa let out a deep sigh. "You'll need to teach that one some tact, Krayden. Or someone with less restraint than Gage here will take the matter into their own hands." Krayden nodded.

"I have tried to convey to her that not every thought in her head needs to be spoken but my advice has yet to take root. Now, I don't imagine you are here just to pick up Mr. Grant's package? I doubt you would come for such an errand." He looked at Gage as he said the last. Gage confirmed that with a nod.

"Well then, hmm. What can I do for you?" Gage nodded at Lissa. It was her lead after all, and she had yet to share it with him.

"We have reason to believe that a man who goes by the name of Bull may have some information we are after. Do you know anything of him?"

"Hmm, come on into the back. I keep notes on people of interest, but I can tell you now that the name does ring a bell." Krayden set a wooden sign in the front window indicating the shop was closed, locked the front door, and led them into the back.

Krayden walked over to a small, wooden desk set against the back wall. The rest of the room was full of small tables covered in glassware full of different powders and liquids. A small brazier was lit in one corner and a hearth, unlit, was set in another. A set of stairs led down to the basement, a rare thing in this city, and another led to the second floor. The walls were full of shelves that housed a seemingly endless variety of herbs and medicines.

"Hmm, yes, here it is. According to my intelligence, this 'Bull' is new to the city. He has been here for about a month and already has a reputation for nasty work." Krayden continued scanning the page.

"Specialty?" Gage spoke for the first time since entering the shop. Most Narcomancers had a specialty. There was a myriad of reasons for why they tended to gravitate toward specific drugs. Over time, Narcomancers tended to garner a reputation for specific substances and their accompanying skills.

"Ah, alcohol for sure. Hmm, but some reports indicate he may use others as well. Can't confirm if he's a true Blender." Gage nodded at that. It was often difficult to identify if someone was a Blender. People tended to focus on the detail that stood out most and that could lead to inaccurate reports.

"Where can we find him?" Lissa asked.

"Well, hmm, according to my notes, he's known to hang around Tricks. But he's been seen around Mills as well. Hmm, bad news, bad news, that."

Gage knew that Krayden was right. Mills was bad for anyone who didn't live there. The gang that ran it, the Breakers, were as powerful as the Fangs, but far more ruthless. They would be better served approaching him somewhere in Tricks.

"We'll have to get him in Tricks, then." Lissa echoed his thoughts. Gage couldn't help but feel proud that she had grown so well after moving on from his tutelage. Few people probably remembered that he had been the one to take her as an apprentice when she had first arrived in the city. Just a thin stick of a girl fresh from the grand city of Il Darra down in Lo Darash. She was a true Narcomancer now, skilled and intelligent.

"Description?" Halfjaw asked.

"Hmm, tall, fairly well built. Dark hair, tan skin and a scar across his nose."

"Not too much to go on." Lissa put in.

"Should be enough." Halfjaw said, decisively.

"Yes, well, is there anything else you need from me?" Krayden asked.

"Just the package for Grant," Lissa answered. "And then, I suppose I'll have to wait for Dane."

"I'm done here." Gage looked at Lissa. "I'll meet you at the Pipe tonight. We'll talk about finding Bull." Lissa nodded and Gage turned to leave.

He left the shop and walked with purpose toward the nearest leatherworker. Gage typically liked to work only with people he knew personally, but in this case, his needs were simple. His tongue probed at the side of his mouth as he walked. He had been caught unaware by those Lurchers that night. His years of simple guard duty had made him complacent. Never again.

He entered the shop, the smell of tanning oil and old leather hit him instantly. He approached the counter where a man was working on what looked like an old bridle. The man looked up as Gage approached.

"I need something made. Custom."

"What is it and how soon?" The old man looked at him appraisingly. It was likely he would recognize Gage, but if he did, he gave no sign of it. Smart man.

"Black leather bag. Thick enough to be hard to cut through. Big enough to fit a man's head, with a good, strong drawstring." Gage took a moment before continuing. Talking was a chore for him. "Need it by tomorrow morning."

"Uh, well, I got some good Marthen leather in," the old man said. "Lurcher stuff. Takes a good deal of sawing with a keen blade to get through. Rush job is gonna cost though."

"How much?" The man pulled out a sheet of paper and did some quick sums.

"Three silver, seven copper marks." A fair sum, but well within Gage's means.

"Done." He shook the man's hand and left the shop. He turned back toward his apartment. He needed to study those documents again and maybe ask around more about this "Bull". Whoever he was, he was likely dangerous, and Gage intended to be well prepared for him. Most people assumed you couldn't kill a Narcomancer while he had alcohol in him, but Gage knew a way. And when he found the men who had robbed him and killed Faron, he would use it.

Chapter 6

Dane followed Tally down the stairs to the basement. The steps were narrow and steep, ending abruptly at a thick door with a heavy padlock on it. Tally pulled a heavy iron key from her pocket and unlocked the lock. She pushed open the door and stepped inside. As Dane stepped inside the dark room, Tally bustled around lighting oil lamps at each corner.

As light flared to life, Dane saw what the room contained. Floor to ceiling shelves held row after row of glass jars, each labeled with a small piece of paper. He had never imagined that such a quantity of drugs existed in all the world, let alone some cramped basement room in the slums of Alcaren. There was a small table in the center of the room, with two tiny chairs on either side. Tally sat in one of the chairs and indicated that Dane should have the other.

After he took his seat, Tally cleared her throat and began to speak. "So, how much do you know about Narcomancy? It's good to get a baseline of your knowledge before I begin as I tend to ramble once I get going." She chuckled as she met Dane's eyes. He reflexively looked down at the table.

"Not much, really. Almost nothing." He was ashamed of his lack of knowledge, though how he could be expected to know anything about the most secretive group of people in the world was unclear. Tally did not seem disappointed in his response, however.

"No matter. Most of the new ones don't know much. Let's just start with what you do know."

"Well, I know alcohol makes you invincible—" Tally immediately cut him off.

"Not invincible. Impervious is a better word for it. You can't be physically harmed, but you can be stopped. You could be immobilized or imprisoned until the alcohol wears off." She paused then, seeming to realize that she had interrupted him. "Sorry, dear. Continue."

"Um, coccin gives you strength and speed." He looked up at her and when he saw she was not going to talk over him again, he went on, eyes lowered. "Baccin makes you see better, I think.

Cannin has something to do with tricking people, but I don't really know how. And poprin is for healing." He looked back up.

"Is that all?"

"Um, yes."

"Not a bad base for a start, though there are some misconceptions in what you've said." She pulled a small leather bag from the nearest shelf. From that bag, she pulled out several glass vials. She held up the first one, which was filled with a white powder. "This is coccin. You are right to say it grants speed and strength. However, there are drawbacks to this. While it makes you a Rager, it does not make you impervious like alcohol. In a hand-to-hand fight, you will most likely be fine with any kind of strike. However, if you are fighting someone wearing armor, you could cause serious harm if you were to, say, punch someone in the breastplate. You would probably injure them, but you would also crush your hand in doing so."

She pulled the cork from the vial and handed it to him. "Don't try to use it here. Just try to familiarize yourself with the look and scent of it." Dane took it and held it up to his eye. "Coccin, along with its Narcomantic effects, also causes an intense surge in emotion. This is why most people who specialize in it are known as Ragers. It can be euphoric, but it also leads to overconfidence and a lack of practicality." Dane nodded and then hesitantly held the vial up to his nose.

"Why do I need to know what it smells like?" He noticed a faint fruit-like scent coming from the vial.

"Well, dear, the sort of business that you're becoming involved in tends to make enemies. That's why there are gangs. To protect each other and work together. It was a common practice years ago, before people like Krayden and myself got involved in the business, to poison another Narcomancer's stash. Or even to just switch one drug for another. Smells are much harder to fake than looks."

Dane found the idea of someone poisoning him terrifying and made sure to note the exact scent. He went to hand it back to Tally, but she shook her head.

"That is yours. There should be enough there for a good amount of practice." She picked up another vial.

"I'm afraid I can't pay for this." He placed the vial on the table. Tally chuckled.

"No worry there, dear. Mr. Grant is paying for this. He covers the costs of all his new Narcomancers. No doubt you'll pay it back soon enough." She shook the vial in her hand. "This is baccin. It does enhance your sight, but that is only a small part of what it does. It magnifies all your senses. Sight, hearing, smell, touch, taste. Even balance, coordination, and other things like that. It's very handy when used with coccin or alcohol. It won't offset the drunkenness or level you out completely, but it will help."

She handed the baccin to Dane. This was something he was familiar with. Many people use baccin just for smoking or chewing. He knew its scent and the texture of the leaves. Tally picked up the next vial, which looked like a different sort of leaf.

"This is cannin. Its uses do involve tricking people, but it can be used in various other ways.

Cannin allows you to affect another person's mind. I've heard it can be tricky to master, although you have the right teacher for that. By all accounts, Miss Lissa is one of the best Foggers in the city." She handed over that vial too. Dane had smelled cannin before. It had a similar earthy scent to baccin, though it was different. Heavier, more pungent.

"This," Tally held up another vial, this one with a small amount of brown powder, "is poprin. You said poprin is used for healing and you're sort of right. It can be used for healing. However, that is not what it does. Poprin allows a Narcomancer to manipulate their physiology." Tally noticed the look of confusion on Dane's face. "That means they can change things about their body. It's very difficult to use and incredibly addictive. I would suggest avoiding using it unless you have no choice." This vial she tucked back into the leather pouch. "It is also dangerous in that it has no scent of its own, though that makes it harder to hide another substance mixed in it."

She stood, walked to the back of the room, picked up a small jar, and returned to the table with it. She pulled out the large cork and pulled out a small disk-like thing. It looked soft to the touch and smelled very strongly of dirt.

"This is psylin. It is incredibly rare. This jar is all we have of it." She placed the psylin back in the jar. "It comes from a mushroom that grows only in the caves of the Misty Vale, up in the north of Yoshir."

"What does it do?"

"Well dear, it supposedly lets you see the future." Dane's eyes went wide. What would it be like to know the future? To know exactly what would come each day? A man could get rich easily on that.

"I know what you're thinking, but this is Narcomancy, dear. It's not that easy." She sighed and looked him in the eye. "The visions granted by psylin are often confusing and difficult to understand. It also requires a great deal of it to provide any lasting visions." Dane was disappointed to hear that, though he supposed it made sense. If it were easy, it wouldn't be such a secret.

"Now, we need to talk about the cost of these substances. As I said, poprin is the most addictive and hardest to use. I would recommend staying away from it unless your life is on the line."

She got up and crossed the room, returning the jar of psylin to its shelf. "Baccin is the least harmful for long-term use. As I'm sure you know, many people use it daily for their entire lives. There are some potential hazards though. The rot can get into your mouth, jaw, tongue, or lungs in time. Even with poprin, these things are incurable, except in rare circumstances.

"Cannin has few drawbacks as well, though some say prolonged use can dull your mind. Even to the point of losing all will to perform daily functions." Tally returned to her seat. "Now, coccin and alcohol are generally manageable, to some extent. They are the most dangerous in two ways. The first is that they are very easy to overdose on. Especially in a fight. Your body won't be able to tell you that you have had too much when your mind is telling you that you need more to continue fighting. Coccin is notorious for this, though it is common with alcohol as well.

"The second is that their long-term use effects are irreversible and deadly. Using these substances causes damage to many of your internal organs. They're bad enough for normal people, but even more so for Narcomancers. This is also why it is unwise to use multiple substances at once. It can be done, but it is very dangerous."

"Why is it worse for us?" Dane had lost his wonder at the psylin and was now feeling less and less happy about his newfound status. It seemed that every one of these things that gave him power was also capable of killing him with no hope of averting it. "And if it is possible to mix them, then why is it so unwise?"

"So far as we can tell, based on autopsies and other studies, a normal person's body uses a couple of key organs to process these substances. This takes time and is done at a cost. But Narcomancers are able to force their bodies to process them at much faster rates. This puts a tremendous amount of stress upon the body. It is the main reason why few of them live past forty years. Between the addictions themselves and the stress of their use," Tally shrugged her shoulders, "it's just too much. As for mixing substances, it is done fairly often, but rarely well. We call such people Blenders. Baccin is safe to use with just about anything else, cannin too. But mixing coccin and alcohol is exceedingly dangerous due to their hazardous short-term effects and the amount of each that must be consumed."

"I didn't realize so few of us lived that long." The dangers of mixing made some sense to Dane, but he was shocked by the short lifespan. His father was already fifty. To think Dane himself might never come close to that age made him feel as if his life were already half over.

"There are ways around it." Tally lifted Dane's chin, so he had no choice but to meet her eyes again. "You don't need to use these gifts. Learn enough to control them and then go far away and find a normal life." She let go of his chin and sat back. "Or you can try to find the middle ground. Many do though most fail. Pursue your career as a Narcomancer but hold off the addictions as much as possible. That's how Lissa and Old Halfjaw get by. They use the substances only when they need to. At some point, it will get too much for them and they will need to try to quit. This is where most people fail."

"And poprin can't heal these kinds of afflictions? The failing organs and the rots?"

"Dear, have you not been listening? Poprin is the most dangerous of these drugs. If you tried to use it to revive your failing organs, you would surely overdose in the process. Even closing a cut requires a fair amount of the stuff. Fixing things that our best medicines cannot mend? Your body wouldn't even be able to handle the drug long enough to take advantage of the power." Tally looked at him with sympathy. "I have shown you your paths. Which you choose and how you tread it is up to you now."

Dane nodded. Tally seemed satisfied, rose from her seat, and turned toward another shelf. She grabbed a smaller, empty leather pouch and a large bottle of clear liquid.

"Here." She held them out to him. "A nice pouch for your substances. And a bottle of grain liquor." She eyed him sitting there, staring at the large bottle, wondering how he was supposed to walk around with that. She suddenly shook her head and grabbed a larger sack off the shelf. "Of course, you can't go carrying that through the streets. How silly of me." She handed him the sack and he stuffed the bottle into it.

Dane was about to get up when a thought occurred to him. "Are these all the drugs there are?" Tally looked at him thoughtfully.

"Well, dear, so far as we know they are the only ones that grant abilities. There are other recreational drugs, and some medicines that people abuse. But for our purposes, yes. These are the only ones.

"There are legends of another drug that was said to allow a Narcomancer to control another person's mind. It was made from a rare plant found only in the ruins of Old Marth. However, there is no evidence to suggest that they are real. Most historians agree that the tales come from exaggerated reports of talented Foggers." Dane nodded at that and followed as Tally led him out the door and back up the stairs.

Dane found Lissa sitting in the back room waiting for him. "Do you think you've got a grasp on things?" she asked as he aproached her.

"I think I understand the basics, though I have no idea what any of it actually feels like. Other than alcohol."

"Good." Lissa said farewell to Krayden, who was bent over a worktable and Tally, then walked out to the front of the shop. Dane followed her out through the front and onto the street.

"What do we do now?" Dane asked.

"We'll get you set up with a couple of other dopemages from the gang to live with. They'll keep an eye on you and help you with some of the basics until I have time to focus on you properly. Hopefully my business with Halfjaw will be done in a few days."

Dane nodded at that. It would be nice to have a place to live again. As they walked back toward Hollows, he mulled over everything he had learned. He had a decision to make now. Back out and leave this dangerous business behind or commit and do his best to hold onto life for as long as he could.

Chapter 7

Lissa led Dane through the maze of the slums with little conversation. Dane seemed lost in thought, which she understood. She well remembered her own basic instructions with Tally. It was a lot of information to process, especially for a kid. Still, dopemages couldn't afford coddling. He would have to learn fast, another aspect of her training that she remembered well.

They were just back inside the boundaries of Hollows when Dane spoke up. "So, what am I to do until you're ready to teach me?" It was a fair question, though he asked it timidly.

"I know a couple of trustworthy men you can live with for now. They're veterans with good heads on their shoulders." It was true, though most dopemages who reached twenty had good heads on their shoulders as a matter of necessity. Storr and Tamar were about as good a pair as could be found in Alcaren. "They'll teach you a few things and see you stay out of trouble."

That seemed a good enough answer for now, as Dane said nothing more. The sun was almost to the horizon when they reached a street full of tenements and the occasional house. Houses were rare things in the slums, and most were used as apartments. The house Lissa led Dane to was not one of these. It was a squat two-story building made of wood with a stone chimney on one side. It was not particularly well made, but by the standards of the slums it was a nice place.

Lissa strode up to the front door and let herself in without knocking. Dane followed her inside, slowly. Two men sat on chairs on either side of a small table, one with dice in his hand, the other holding a pipe to his lips. They both looked up simultaneously, relaxing when they saw it was her.

"Lissa." The man with dice in his hand, Tamar, greeted her with a nod. He was a tall, thin Darashi man with short black hair and dark, serious eyes. The other man was more animated. He smiled at her, his blue eyes bright. Storr was an amiable man from somewhere in New Marth. His curly brown hair fell just above his eyes and his slight frame was almost lost in the baggy shirt and trousers he wore.

"Been a long time since you've stopped by!" Storr said, rising. "Too rich to take a smoke with your old pals?" He wagged his finger at her playfully.

"I'm only rich because I avoid gambling with the likes of you two." Lissa replied. "As for the smoke, I simply haven't had much time of late."

"Too busy helping the Halfjaw, yes?" Tamar asked from where he sat. He spoke in a deliberate manner, his Darashi accent more apparent than her own.

"You've heard about that?" Lissa was not surprised; it was big news whenever something like this happened. Particularly if it happened to a man of Halfjaw's reputation.

"Whole city has, I expect." Storr put in. "And who's that there by the door?" He peered around her to look at Dane.

"This is Dane." Lissa turned and motioned the boy forward. "He is the reason I'm here. New recruit to the gang, new to Narcomancy. Just need you to look after him for a bit, maybe show him the ropes until my business with Halfjaw is finished."

"You dice, boy?" Storr asked immediately. "We enjoy a game now and then if you're interested." He had a sly smile on his face. Dane shook his head, looking down at the floor. Lissa gave Storr a sharp look, before turning her attention to Dane.

"They're good enough men and they'll treat you fine. But don't gamble with them or they'll take everything you've got." Dane nodded at that. Lissa forced herself not to sigh. The boy needed to learn to speak more. She addressed the two men instead of letting her frustration show. "Be good to him. I'll stop by in a few days, and we'll work out a more permanent arrangement." With that, she turned back to the door to leave.

"Is that it, then?" Storr called to her. "Leavin' just like that?" Lissa turned back to face the jolly little man.

"That's it, Storr. I'm a busy woman."

"Come on in boy, have a seat!" Storr said to Dane. "Call me Storr, and that there, is Tamar. No need to worry, we don't bite!" Dane shuffled further into the sitting room.

"Not unless you ask nicely." Tamar put in with a straight face. Storr chuckled at that.

Lissa could hear Storr begin to pepper Dane with questions before she was out the door. It would be good for the kid to be around someone like Storr. It would force him to speak more and open up.

She headed for the Pipe to meet back up with Halfjaw. It would take some careful planning to deal with this Bull fellow. Whether he was one of the men involved in the theft or just someone in the know, he would likely be inclined to fight or run before talking.

Halfjaw wasn't at the Pipe when she arrived, so she headed toward the back office. Dosk let her pass, as usual, and she found Grant in his typical spot behind the large desk. As always, he had a glass of whiskey in front of him.

"I trust you have my package?" He did not bother with an introduction, which was fine with Lissa. She wasn't one for formalities and was eager to get back out front to wait for Halfjaw. She reached into her jacket and pulled out the small, wrapped package, placing it on the desk.

"Excellent!" He began unwrapping it, not bothering to wait for her to leave. She was glad of that, as she had been quite curious as to what had him so eager. "Did things go alright with the new boy?"

"A typical first-timer, I think. I set him up with Storr and Tamar for now." Grant nodded at that as he pulled the object from the wrapping. It was something strange. A glass cylinder attached to a metal part that extended in a needle-like spike. "What is that sir?"

He glanced at her, a sly smile on his toad-like face. He turned it over in his hands carefully; it looked very delicate.

"The future, Lissa." His smile grew. "This is the future. It is a new design of Krayden's. He calls it a syringe. You see, you put a liquidized form of a drug in this glass part, then stick the needle into one of your veins. A very delicate process I'm told. Then you push down on this part, and it injects the drug directly into your blood. Supposedly, this greatly increases the potency of the substance."

Lissa was stunned. Drugs that could be placed directly in the blood would mean a lot of changes. "That sounds unbelievable sir." Grant placed it carefully back on the desk.

"Yes, it does." He continued to admire the device. "But Krayden has assured me that it has been tested extensively." He looked back up at her. "Do you fully understand what this means, Lissa?"

"Perhaps, though I think not entirely."

"Money, Lissa. Lots and lots of money." His smile widened and the greed on his face was plain. But there was something more, a kind of hunger. There was more to this than just money; Grant had plenty of that. Perhaps he hoped to control the trade of this thing. But something told her it was more than that. There was no point in asking, however. He would tell her when he wanted her to know and not a moment before.

Lissa excused herself and Grant let her go with a wave of his hand. She returned to the front of the tavern and found Halfjaw sitting at a booth in the far corner, facing the door. She grabbed a drink from the bar and seated herself across from him.

"So, got a plan for tomorrow?"

"Somewhat," Halfjaw explained the beginnings of his plan. Lissa would approach Bull and try to get what information she could out of him. Halfjaw would keep watch from afar and only intervene if things got violent.

"And if he runs rather than talking?" Lissa asked.

"You let him go," Halfjaw answered, "and I tail him back to wherever he goes." It was a simple plan, but not a bad one. The only problem was that Halfjaw was not as spry as he had once been.

"I like it, but may I suggest a slight change." He raised an eyebrow at that. "You should chat him up and I should tail him. I'm faster than you and I can use cannin to keep him from noticing me." Halfjaw was already shaking his head before she finished speaking.

"If he was one of the ones involved in the robbery, he'll know my face. It has to be you that approaches him."

"Everyone knows your face. It's one of the more recognizable ones as faces go." Lissa tried to keep the cheek out of her voice, though it was difficult. "Which means it'll be hard to tail him and keep a low profile."

"I'll wear a hood. But low profile or not, it won't matter if we're made from the start."

They continued to argue for some time. Eventually, they agreed that they'd both pursue Bull if he fled. Lissa would tail him and pretend to lose him at some point, lulling him into thinking he had shaken his pursuer. Halfjaw would stay with him until wherever he went to ground.

"What time do we start?" Lissa asked. "And where? We don't know if he has a place of preference or if he just wanders around."

"Noon." Halfjaw said. "We stake out the main roads between Mills and Tricks. We have a description. If we see someone who matches it, we follow. Then we see what we can find out."

It was good enough for Lissa. The Nalathi knew she had done more with less.

"Best get some sleep then."

Chapter 8

Gage leaned against the side of an old building, the sun was directly overhead and fiercely bright. His pipe stuck out from his lips, the smoke curling up in lazy puffs. Lissa leaned next to him, watching the other end of the street. They were positioned on the corner of two of the busiest streets that met the edge where Tricks ended, and Mills began. They had been on watch for several hours already with no sign of Bull.

Gage had not taken any coccin yet, but the urge thrummed through his body. Even though this was more of an information gathering mission, he longed for a fight. He itched to redeem himself. The looming deadline, now two days away, nagged at him as well.

He had been through the boxes of papers still hidden in his apartment, but they had yielded nothing. They appeared to be merchants' reports from around the world and other such accounts of expeditions to far off places. None of them gave any indication who might have ordered the robbery.

Gage couldn't keep his thoughts from the potential of an imminent fight. He had picked up the leather sack earlier that morning and felt better having it tucked into the back of his belt. He was confident that he wouldn't have to use it in a one-on-one fight, but it was better to be prepared.

"How much longer are we going to wait here?" Lissa demanded quietly. It was growing uncomfortably hot, and the building they leaned against offered little shade.

"As long as it takes."

She sighed but made no argument. Gage understood her frustration. She was used to action. Grant gave her a task and she did it, no standing around in the sun on a crowded street, hoping for one person to walk by. Lissa's preferred manner of surveillance was generally done at night and from a comfortable hiding place. But some things couldn't be helped.

The sun drifted across the sky as they continued to wait. Gage was beginning to lose hope when Lissa suddenly stiffened. She poked his arm and nodded at the other side of the street.

Gage's baccin enhanced sight located the man quickly.

He was taller than Gage and more heavily built. The scar on his nose was plain even from a distance. Gage instantly recognized him as one of the men with crossbows who had killed Faron.

"It's him." Gage let Bull pass their position and get a couple dozen feet ahead before he pushed himself off the wall and fell into step behind him. The press of the crowded street made it difficult to keep an eye on the target, but with Lissa to help, it was doable.

"You're sure?" She muttered as she walked with him.

"I recognize him from the robbery." Lissa nodded at that and moved away from him to keep a clear line on Bull.

After a few minutes of walking, Bull turned and entered a grubby-looking tavern. Run-down as it was, it was what passed for decent in this slum. They set up across the street and waited a few more minutes to make sure he was staying. Finally, Lissa nodded at Gage, walked over to the tavern and entered.

Gage pulled a small vial of coccin from his pocket and discreetly snorted it. The dope flooded his system as he activated it, urging him to move, run, fight. It was hard to hold off, but he did. Typically, he wouldn't have taken it until he was sure he needed it, but in this case, he needed to be able to move immediately. A small part of him acknowledged that he also had missed the rush of the drug and was giving in to the craving.

Gage moved across the street and subtly moved to one of the tavern windows. Unlike most taverns in the slums, it had actual glass in the frame, not just open wooden shutters. He peered through the dirty glass pane and located Lissa. She was sitting across a table from Bull. She was drinking whiskey from a small glass while Bull took a long drink from a tall glass of clear liquor.

It was a dangerous situation for Lissa. He wasn't sure what excuse she was using for talking to him, but if he was drinking the strong grain liquor favored by Narcomancers, Lissa would be at a disadvantage with simple whiskey. They talked for a while, Lissa doing most of the talking while Bull answered in short bursts. He had a casual air about him, leaning back in his chair, legs splayed.

Lissa was resting her arms on the table, her body forward.

Gage noticed when the conversation turned. Bull pulled his legs in, his face becoming a mask. Lissa tensed in her seat. The exchange continued for a minute before Bull struck.

Bull exploded into motion at a speed that had to be fueled by coccin. His hands gripped the table and flung it upward into Lissa's face too fast for her to counter. The table struck her and threw her back across the tavern, out of sight. Gage was about to hurl himself through the window and help, but Bull was already moving toward the front door. He was fleeing, not looking to continue the fight.

Gage decided Lissa would have to fend for herself. He needed to take this opportunity to follow Bull. He slipped around the corner of the building and waited for Bull to run by. He had barely gotten himself out of sight when Bull ran by. He was no longer moving unnaturally fast. Either he had burned up his store of coccin or was saving it up and trying not to draw attention. That would make tailing him easier.

Gage followed Bull through the crowded streets. Few people had taken any notice of the episode at the tavern. Such things were not unheard of in the slums, after all. Even so, Bull had set himself at a reasonably fast, but not unusual pace. Gage matched him, keeping himself about fifty feet behind and to the left. If Bull made a sudden turn or burst into a run Gage could use his coccin to catch up. He would not let the man get away. It was preferable to follow him to his hideout, but taking him captive would be better than losing him.

They soon crossed into Mills. The streets were less clogged with pedestrians, but more crowded with beggars and urchins. Mills was a microcosm of Alcaren itself. Where it was poor, it was the worst of the slums. Homeless people and decrepit, useless buildings were everywhere. But where the gangs made their headquarters, it was among the best areas outside the Heights themselves. The Breakers kept their wealth to themselves, unlike the Fangs. Grant was adamant about keeping Hollows a respectable place, at least by slum standards.

Gage had to be careful about his tailing here. His clothes were noticeably better than almost anyone else's, and there was a greater chance of Bull noticing he was being followed. And, of course, if Bull caught a glimpse of him, he would definitely recognize Gage. Both because he had robbed Gage himself, as well as Gage's distinctive appearance.

Gage was experienced in these matters and kept himself scarce enough that Bull never noticed him. Gage managed to follow him to a large warehouse near the center of Mills. Bull entered immediately, and Gage lingered across the street. He wanted to see if anyone else was coming or going.

Gage waited for almost an hour, and when he saw no one else enter or leave, he moved closer to investigate. He moved up to the large, dirt-stained windows that ran along the side of the building. It took him a few tries to find a view that was clear enough yet allowed him to stay out of direct sight. The interior of the warehouse was wide open. It had piles of crates and boxes stacked all around the sides with a large table positioned in the center. At the table, Bull sat with three other men. He appeared to be telling them about his encounter with Lissa.

A particular sight caught Gage's eye. In the far corner of the warehouse, a pile of boxes looked cleaner than the rest. They were better made and noticeably less worn. Gage immediately recognized them as the boxes stolen from his wagon.

A rush of adrenaline surged through him. He wanted to leap through the window and kill these men right there and then. Gage forced himself to be still. That was foolish. Even if he killed them, he could not transport the boxes of his employer's goods alone. He would need to fall back, check on Lissa and form a plan.

It irked Gage to turn away and head back toward Tricks, but he did it. Lissa found him as soon as he passed into Tricks.

"Did you follow him?" She looked a bit disheveled but uninjured. Gage nodded.

"They have my employer's property at a warehouse near the center of the slum." He looked her over critically. "You okay?"

"Yeah, I had enough alcohol in me that I took no injury. I was held up by the barman trying to 'help' me." She shook her head at that.

114

"How did you approach him and how did it go wrong?"

"I posed as a simple thief looking to join a gang. Told him I'd heard rumors of a big robbery and that I'd like to join if he had more work." She scoffed and pursed her lips. "As for how it went wrong? Better to say it was never right. He didn't buy it from the start." Gage nodded at that.

"Let's head back to the Pipe." He guided her away from the way to Mills. "We need to make a plan for getting my employer's goods back."

Chapter 9

Dane awoke to Storr standing over the pallet of bedding set up for him in a small side room.

"Up you get, kid. Lissa said we're to teach you some basics, so best we get to it." Dane nodded dully and forced himself to rise. He was tired from a late night spent drinking with Storr and Tamar, who lectured him at length on the virtues of gambling. As he entered the kitchen, he saw through the window that it was already nearing noon. Storr pushed a heel of good bread smeared with butter into his hands as he moved past him.

"Come on," Storr said as he pulled the front door open. "You can eat as we walk." Dane wished he could sit and eat, but Lissa had told him to follow these men, so he did as he was told. Tamar was already outside, seated on the stoop and smoking from a pipe made of dark wood. He nodded to Dane as he fell into step beside Storr.

Dane's head pounded as he followed the two men through the streets. He noticed that they soon passed out of the residential area into some sort of warehouse district. Tall, wide buildings dominated the narrow streets, leaving little room for the sun to shine down. They came to one at the end of a dead-end street. This one was larger than the rest. It was five stories tall and at least three hundred feet long.

Storr pushed the front door open without knocking. Dane followed along with Tamar into a small office room. Three men lounged in chairs around a table to one side, while a thin, severe-looking woman sat behind a desk on the other. A large door stood opposite the one they had entered. The men barely glanced at Dane, but the woman looked at him with sharp, blue eyes set deep in her dark-skinned face.

"Got a fresh recruit to work with, Sherim," Storr said to the woman with a smile. She nodded slightly and lowered her head to whatever paperwork she was working on. Tamar nudged Dane in the back, urging him toward the other door. Storr pulled it open as Dane reached it.

"Welcome to your first official day as a Narcomancer." Dane stepped through the door and stared around in awe. The entire interior of the warehouse was one giant room. There were no windows except at the very top of the walls. Wooden platforms ran along the outer edges of the wall at regular story heights, forming a series of balconies that encircled the room.

The center of the room was filled with various structures, some metal, and some wood. There was a series of steps set up on wooden poles that formed a disconnected path around the room. Metal bars hung from the ceiling on ropes in a similar formation.

"What is all this?" Dane asked, still unable to get over his awe.

"This is where we train. We call it the Barn." Storr said. "Each of these serves a purpose to practice with your powers on."

Dane could see now how some of them made sense. The disconnected steps were obviously meant to be run across, probably with baccin, to increase balance and coordination. Others still made no sense, though he was sure he would learn in time. It was a pretty daunting sight.

"Don't worry about all that yet." Storr was smiling at the bemused look on Dane's face.

"Mostly for today, we're gonna work with alcohol. Maybe some baccin." Dane nodded as Storr handed him a flask. Dane forced down two strong pulls of the grain liquor. It burned in his throat, but another part of him felt the rush of power.

"Now there's two ways to really get you used to being a Lurcher. The first is to let you run the obstacle course with no baccin. You will inevitably fall, hard and often. This will allow you to become accustomed to trusting the alcohol and not flinching from things you would expect to hurt." Storr smiled, a glint in his eye as he went on. "The second way is quicker."

"What's that?" Dane asked.

"We beat the piss out of you." Tamar said simply, a small smile pulled at the corner of his mouth. With that he slammed his fist into Dane's gut. Dane doubled over, flinching at the pain he expected to come. It never did, of course. He had enough alcohol in him to withstand just about anything at the moment. "Let us know when you start to feel it. Need to make sure you keep enough booze in you."

The blows continued to come. There was no malice in them, though both men did take some pleasure in it. It took Dane much longer than he would have guessed to accustom himself to it. Although his brain knew nothing they did could hurt him, years of his father's cuffs, slaps, and kicks had seared the expectation of pain into his deepest instincts. Each time he began to feel the effects of the alcohol lessen, he held up his hand and Storr and Tamar would back off so he could take another shot.

Dane lost track of how long it took him to take the blows without flinching. Once it clicked in his mind, he got the knack of it quickly. There was a savage sort of joy in it. Each time they struck him or hurled him around the room, he was able to pop back up, unaffected. Dane could feel the thrill of it now. The confidence of knowing he would never suffer pain at another man's hands was heady.

"I think he's got it now," Storr said, finally. Tamar nodded in agreement. "Time for you to start fighting back." He and Tamar each took shots from their own flasks. Dane wasn't sure what to make of this part. He had fought the occasional scrap back in his village, but those had been brawling, wild events. He had never learned how to properly fight. When Dane mentioned this to Storr, he just chuckled.

"Just do what you can for now. Easier for us to correct what you do wrong after we've seen it."

So, they began to fight. The two men did not gang up on Dane. They fought him one at a time, and Dane could tell they were taking it easy on him. After all, this was not about beating him, but teaching him.

Dane's blows were wild and uncoordinated, not just because of his inexperience but also due to his inebriation. It was difficult to implement the things they taught him when he had such little control of his body.

"Shouldn't I take some baccin? Or wait until I'm sober to learn this stuff?" Dane suggested. Storr shook his head.

"Nah, you need to learn to function in this state. Unless you choose to focus on other substances, you will need to be able to fight competently, and handle yourself while you're this drunk." That made sense to Dane.

After several hours of instruction and sparring, Storr finally called an end to the training. Dane was sweaty and tired but happy that he had sustained not even a single bruise. He stumbled as he walked toward the office door. Storr caught his arm with a chuckle.

"You're gonna need more practice drinking. Gotta get used to functioning while this deep in the bag." Tamar chuckled at that too. Dane saw the wisdom of that, but the warnings about the long-term dangers of such use that Tally had informed him of nagged at his mind. He reminded himself that he had still not committed to this life.

Storr and Tamar led Dane back to the house, where Dane stumbled to his pallet in the small room and promptly fell asleep.

Some hours later, Dane was shaken awake by Storr again.

"Come on, kid. We got somewhere to show you." Dane's head pounded at the sound of Storr's voice. He felt even worse than he had felt that morning. He stumbled into the kitchen again to find food set out on the table. Dane fell to without even asking. He shoved bread and meat into his mouth, only now realizing how hungry he was.

"Slow down, kid." Tamar told him, that half smile again tugging at his mouth. "And take this." He pushed a small glass of whiskey across the table.

"It'll help the hangover." Tamar said when Dane looked at it questioningly. Dane shrugged and downed the liquor. After eating, he realized that he felt much better. Not great, but better. Storr walked back into the room.

"Let's go. Fights start in an hour." Tamar rose immediately and headed for the door.

"What fights?" Dane was suddenly nervous. Did they expect him to join them on some mission already? He was sure he was not ready for that.

"You'll see," Storr said. He seemed to notice the look of trepidation on Dane's face. "Don't worry kid. This is just good old fashioned dopemage fun." Dane decided to trust him and got up to follow.

Storr and Tamar led Dane to an unfamiliar part of the slums. They entered a wide, squat building, Dane following behind the other two men. He heard the crowd before he could see around Tamar and Storr. When he managed to look between them, he noticed they were in a large barroom. It was packed with people.

Storr led them to the bar and ordered three whiskeys. After he got the drinks and distributed them to Tamar and Dane, he led them to the back of the room and through a door. They emerged into a circular room with a large opening in the center.

Dane followed to the edge of the circle and peered over the railing that ran along it. Down in the center was a pit with a sand-covered floor. Two men were in the pit, and as Dane watched, they began to fight. They moved with supernatural speed, striking and parrying over and over in the span of a few seconds.

"What is this?" Dane had to practically shout to be heard over the roar of the crowd.

"This is where dopemages come to make a little extra money," Storr explained. "Fighters can make a lot of money here if they're good. The rest

124

of us make money betting on them." Dane could see why the fights were so popular. The speed and skill exhibited by the two men was mesmerizing. He wondered if he could be like these men someday. Powerful and confident, cheered on by hundreds of screaming admirers. It touched something inside of him that he had never known was there. A part of himself that longed to be respected and maybe, a little feared.

The fight below followed a strange pattern. The two men would come together in a flurry of blows: punching, kicking, dodging, and ducking. This exchange would last a minute or two, then the combatants would retreat several steps each and take another hit of coccin. It didn't make sense to Dane. Why wouldn't they just fight until one of them ran out and then was beaten or forced to submit?

"They fight in the old way," Storr explained when Dane asked. "Supposedly, back in the old days, when Narcomancy was more respected, when two dopemages fought, they would fight like this. Brief, violent clashes that would end when each needed another hit. The loser would be the one who ran out of reserves first. Usually, the loser would submit, sometimes they would insist on fighting to the death, but rarely."

"And these are not fights to the death," Tamar added. "If dopemages died frequently in these fights, they would be stopped; either by the constables or the gangs themselves. We are too precious a resource, yes?" Dane could think of nothing to add, so he just nodded. Tamar's Darashi accent made it difficult to tell sometimes if he was actually asking a question. The fight down below ended abruptly as one of the men caught the other in a hold and bent him toward the ground. The crowd roared as the caught man tapped his submission.

They stood at the railing, nursing their drinks through several more fights. They saw Lurchers against Lurchers, fighting with long thick cudgels. Ragers, like the first two, fought in a flurry of motion that was difficult to follow. They even saw one instance of a Lurcher against a Rager that ended with the Rager being struck a savage blow by the Lurcher's cudgel.

"Lucky strike!" Storr shouted as the crowd roared around them. He turned to Dane. "Tamar and I need to go see someone about placing a few bets. Stay here alright?" Dane nodded and looked back down to the pit, where the Rager was being helped out by two other men.

Dane looked around while the next fight was being arranged. The crowd was a raucous bunch, and all looked much the same. Dirty, unkempt people who came to watch something violent that they could never hope to match in their simple lives. All their faces blended together to Dane.

Except one.

Dane noticed him with a start. Iron grey hair and beard framed a face with dark eyes. He stood across the circle from Dane, the man who had freed him from his father's cellar. Dane stood, paralyzed. He had never expected to see the man again, yet here he was. The man's eyes met Dane's. A small smile appeared on his otherwise inscrutable face. He nodded his head toward the left side of the circle. The crowd was thinner there, and there were tables set against the back wall on that side. The man started making his way there without waiting to see Dane's reaction.

Dane wasn't sure why, but he found himself forcing his way through the crowd to meet the man. As he reached the area the man had indicated, Dane saw him already seated at a table. Dane approached and took a seat across from him.

"Hello, Dane." The strange man looked at him intensely. Dane nodded back, unable to find his voice. "It's nice to see you've gotten as far as I had hoped you might."

"What do you mean?" Dane forced the words out. He hadn't thought much about this man since the night he had been freed. But now, sitting across from him, he remembered how immense the man's presence was. It was not a physical thing, but it loomed large just the same.

"Exactly as I said. I had hoped you would find a life here, and you have. And with one of the most prosperous and influential gangs in the city." The man stared at Dane with those eyes like obsidian.

"Is that all you hoped for me?" Dane wasn't sure why, but he felt, somehow, that this man was very dangerous.

"No," the man said after a pause. "I actually have a favor to ask of you."

"What kind of favor?"

"Nothing extraordinary. A simple theft." Those dark eyes continued to bore into Dane's. There was something about them. Something old.

"Who would I be stealing from? And what?" Dane had never stolen anything other than his father's whiskey. But the thrill of realizing his powers had stuck with him from earlier, and he felt more confident than he had before.

"A simple letter. A letter currently held in a box of goods located in the apartment of a man named Harlon Gage. Also known as 'Halfjaw'." The man said it as if it was a trifling thing, but Dane's blood turned cold. This man wanted him to steal from Halfjaw? All his newfound confidence evaporated. His one encounter with Halfjaw was enough to convince him that man was not one to cross.

"I can't do that." The man sighed, his dark eyes closing briefly.

"I'm afraid I'm not asking." The man's voice was gentle, but there was a firmness to it that would brook no argument. "You see, you owe. I did you a favor. I granted you freedom. You will either return the favor by doing what I ask, or I will take your freedom away." He said it with no heat or force but there was an element of iron to it. A simple force of inevitability. This man knew it would be as he said.

"Can I think about it?" Dane wasn't sure what else to do but play for time.

"I am leaving the city in two days. If you do not bring me the letter I need before then, I will be forced to make other arrangements. Arrangements that you will not enjoy." Dane suppressed a shiver, but he could not ignore the fear he felt creeping up his spine.

"How will I know which letter it is?"

"It will be addressed to a man named Waylan, and it will speak of an expedition to Old Marth. That is all the information you need. Take the letter, nothing else. Then deliver it to me. I will be available at an inn called the Tilted Crown in Arches. Tell the doorman you wish to speak to

Isar." With that, the man got up and slipped away through the crowd.

Dane had no idea what he was going to do. If he was caught by Halfjaw, he had no idea what the man would do. But if he didn't even attempt it, this Isar would exact his own form of revenge. Unsure of what to do, Dane set off through the crowd to find Storr and Tamar.

Chapter 10

The night was clear and the light of the two moons illuminated the street well. Lissa and Halfjaw sat atop a building across from the warehouse that Halfjaw had followed Bull to. Each of them smoked baccin, Lissa from a cigarette, Halfjaw from his new, plain brown pipe. Halfjaw had wanted to bust in and take out the men guarding the place, but Lissa had insisted on staking the place out first.

Everything was quiet, there was no sign of anyone coming or going from the warehouse, nor had there been for hours. The last movement they had seen was the shift change of the men on guard. If the men they had seen were the only ones, then there were only four on watch. That was a manageable number for the two of them.

"What do you think?" Lissa asked. Halfjaw looked at her briefly, then turned his attention back to the warehouse.

"Seems doable."

"Perhaps too doable?" Lissa let her skepticism show in her voice. This all seemed too easy.

"Perhaps." Halfjaw continued to stare down at the building. She could feel his eagerness to act and guessed he had already taken some coccin. She wondered at the level of addiction someone his age must be fighting. He had been a Narcmancer for almost twenty years, a long time for one like them. Lissa herself had only been aware of her powers for about eight years and she was already dealing with intense cravings and looked for excuses to indulge in her powers. She managed them well enough and despite being just twenty-two, she was considered a seasoned veteran. Although, a lot of that could be attributed to having had a good teacher.

Lissa thought back to when she had first come to Alcaren. Her experience had been much like Dane's. Fleeing a hostile place for somewhere she might be allowed to be herself. Instead of cowering on the streets like Dane, she had taught herself to steal. She stole small amounts of baccin and cannin, experimenting with them on her own to accentuate the newfound proclivity she had for thievery.

133

Until one night, she tried to steal from the wrong person. When Halfjaw caught her breaking into his apartment, instead of killing her or turning her in to the constables, he took her on as an apprentice. He had taught her well. He showed her the finer points of the drugs she already had, as well as introducing her to alcohol and cocaine. He drilled into her head the need for discipline. Many talented Narcomancers had fallen victim to the lure of pleasure their tools offered.

Halfjaw had changed since he took a private job for his mysterious merchant employer. He spoke less and never smiled. He never showed a hint of pain but there was no way the old wound his face could be painless.

"You never told me what happened to your face." Lissa made it a statement, implying she didn't need an answer. The look he gave her made it plain that she wouldn't get one.

"Must have been a talented fighter to catch you like that. Or just very lucky." She continued on, knowing he wouldn't give in. But it had been years since they'd spoken, and she felt it was time to at least bring it up. His attention was back on the street, acting as if he hadn't heard her.

"Can't even give me a hint, huh?" Lissa was not disappointed. It was how Halfjaw was now, not that he'd ever been loose lipped. Something in her voice got to him though. For he managed to grunt out a reply.

"I had the rot." He kept his eyes forward, acting as if the admission were all the explanation necessary. Lissa was stunned.

"What do you mean *had*? You can't get rid of the rot." Everyone knew that. The rot was usually caused by baccin, particularly the chewing kind. It could manifest in the cheek or lips. Or sometimes in the jawbone itself.

"Early-stage rot can be cut out."

"Someone cut part of your jaw off?" Lissa could not wrap her mind around that. The pain involved would have been unbearable. And there was no way such an invasive thing could heal as well as his wound had. It clicked in her head then.

"You used poprin, didn't you?" Halfjaw kept his eyes fixed downward. He had always been firmly against messing with poprin. It was dangerous and more addictive than any of the other drugs they used. Not to mention, difficult to use. "So, what went wrong?"

"Wrong?" There was a hint of dismay in his voice. "It went as well as could be expected. Better even."

"But you clearly failed to regrow the jawbone." He finally looked at her, his mouth hanging slightly ajar.

"Regrow the bone?" He shook his head. "The amount of poprin it would take to regrow a bone would have killed me in minutes."

"But poprin is used to mend bones all the time."

"Mend yes. A cracked bone can be sealed with a reasonable amount of it. Not that I consider any amount 'reasonable'. But to regrow a part that was removed would take so much that I would've overdosed in minutes."

"Then why use it at all if you couldn't fix the bone?"

"Soft tissue is much more malleable than bone. I closed the cut from the surgery, which was hard enough. Then Krayden showed me a surgical book that detailed the tendons, ligaments, and muscles of the face. I rearranged them and lengthened them to connect the shortened portion of my jaw to my skull." Lissa was astounded. This was so much different than any rumor or guess that she had ever heard regarding how he might have been injured. Instead, he had nearly succumbed to one of the most common ailments among Narcomancers.

"That sounds difficult." He nodded slowly.

"And painful."

They both fell silent and turned their full attention back to the warehouse. Nothing had changed down there. Lissa couldn't help feeling that a lot had changed on their roof. The things Halfjaw had told her were hard to swallow. But there was a seed of hope in them as well. He had overcome something that had always been regarded as a slow death sentence; perhaps there were other ailments that could be solved as well. Even at such a high price.

Movement caught her eye. She looked down to see two men sneaking along the shadows toward their building. Halfjaw had noticed them too. He leaned over the edge of the building and looked straight down.

"Three Hells!" He swore. Lissa joined him looking down. A group of at least a dozen men were crowded under their building. They immediately noticed their cover was blown and began to beat down the door.

"What do we do?" Before the question was even out of her mouth, Halfjaw was snorting a large dose of coccin and pulling a flask from his belt. He downed the whole thing in one enormous gulp, not even a flinch at the fiery liquor. He pulled another flask from his belt and offered it to her. She shook her head as she pulled her own flask out and took a large swig. Halfjaw took a large puff off his pipe, dumped the burned baccin out and tucked it away. Lissa flicked her nearly spent cigarette away.

"We wait for them to enter, and as they're coming up, we leap down to the street. Then we run." Halfjaw laid out the plan as Lissa took a small hit of coccin. She was not practiced at Blending, but from what they knew of these people, it would be needed tonight. She nodded acceptance at his idea. It was as sound as could be hoped for.

The sound of the heavy oak door below shattering was like a crack of thunder in the clear, quiet night. Lissa pulled out a short cannin cigarette, lit it and puffed hard. She wasn't overly fond of fighting, but she had skills and had developed her own unique way of employing them over the years.

They could hear the rumble of footsteps racing through the building below. Halfjaw peeked over the edge and grunted.

"Five still down there. We'll have to deal with them quickly or the others will just come back down after us." Lissa nodded again, pulling more and more cannin smoke into her lungs.

"Ready?" Halfjaw asked. Lissa nodded as the cannin cigarette burned down to the end. Halfjaw threw himself off the edge of the building, but Lissa waited. She could hear the footsteps getting closer and closer. The door to the roof burst open and the seven other men streamed onto the roof. Lissa harnessed the cannin flooding in through her blood and blasted a command into the men's minds.

We are here. See us and fight us.

She caught a glimpse of their momentarily confused faces as she threw herself backwards over the lip of the building. If her ploy worked well, they would all spend the next several minutes swinging at air across the roof, fighting phantom versions of herself and Halfjaw.

Lissa managed to turn herself in the air so that she landed feet down, the force of the fall sending her to her knees. She was unhurt but a bit disoriented by the fall. She looked around to survey the fight. Halfjaw had driven the five men away from the building, into the street. The fact that any of them were alive was evidence enough that they were at least well imbibed with alcohol.

Halfjaw fought like a whirlwind. Moving as fast as thought, he struck each enemy again and again, leaping from one to the next, hurling them to the ground or tossing them in the air like dolls. But each one rose again, unhurt. Occasionally, one of them would land a blow on Halfjaw, who didn't bother with any sort of defensive moves. He took the blows but by the way they rocked him, they

140

must be using coccin as well. They were Blenders, not as talented as Halfjaw, but dangerous all the same.

Lissa drew upon the rest of her cannin reserve and touched each of their minds.

There are six of us.

She noticed that they all paused, mouths agape as the image of six figures instead of two appeared before them. Halfjaw took the opportunity to pull another flask from his belt and down it without hesitation. She couldn't help but flinch. He was going to feel that tomorrow. He bounded back into the fray, striking more and more wildly as the alcohol overcame the enhanced senses of the baccin he had smoked earlier. They needed to get out of here now.

Lissa raced forward, activated the coccin in her system for the first time. She was not used to the enhanced speed and had to move deliberately. After each time Halfjaw threw a man to the ground, Lissa sprang on the man and disabled him. The first one, she tied his hands behind his back with her belt. The second, she wrapped her cloak around his head and knotted it with the ends tight enough to hold it there. By the third one, she didn't have many options, so she got creative. She took her belt knife and slashed the man's pants along the seams, then pulled them down and twisted them about his ankle. She looked up in time to see Halfjaw grip a man by the arm and leg, then hurl him into the air toward the roof they had been spying from. The fifth man lay dead in the gutter, his neck twisted at an odd angle. His supply of alcohol must have run out.

Shouts from the roof indicated they were beginning to get over her Hazing. Lissa looked to Halfjaw who was moving toward the struggling men on the ground.

"No time Gage!" She hissed at him. "We need to flee! I'll come to you tomorrow, but for now, get out of here!" She waited until he looked at her and nodded his assent. By unspoken agreement, they each fled in a separate direction.

Lissa's feet were dragging by the time she reached her apartment back in Hollows. The loss of the highs from the various drugs was an exhausting sensation. It was as if there were less of something in the world. Her eyes were heavy as she stumbled into her bedroom and collapsed onto the bed. She barely had the energy to pull her boots off before she passed out.

Chapter 11

Gage awoke to a pounding head and bright sunlight streaming in through the window. It was almost noon already. It had been a long time since he had drunk as much as he had the night before. He dragged himself out of bed and forced himself to eat a bland breakfast of buttered bread and porridge. He gulped water until he felt he would burst, but the vicious hangover persisted. Some things couldn't be helped. Fortunately, this particular something could be. He went to his liquor cabinet, pulled out a bottle of Penluck Rye whiskey, and poured a generous glass.

Gage took a sip as he sat, savoring the burn as the liquor ran down his throat and settled warmly in his stomach. He sat in one of the two chairs in his apartment's sitting room, finally relaxing as the whiskey took the edge off his headache.

He thought back to the night before, mulling over the farce their surveillance mission had devolved into. He mentally kicked himself for allowing Lissa to distract him with her questions about his jaw. He still wasn't sure why he had even told her the truth when he had kept it secret from everyone else, except Krayden.

A loud knocking on his door interrupted his moment of peace and brought the headache back twice as bad as before. Gage stumbled to his feet grumbling angrily as he went to answer it.

Lissa pushed through as soon as he turned the knob. She stalked about the apartment, clearly out of sorts.

"Last night was a disaster!" She was fuming. Again, it was startling to Gage how closely her mindset aligned with his own. "We are too good at this to let a bunch of thugs corner us!" Gage could do no more than shrug at that. He didn't want to place the blame on her for distracting him. He found his seat again, picking up the glass of rye and taking a sip.

"Bit early for that, huh?" Lissa eyed him uncertainly. She knew it was unusual for him to resort to drinking like this.

"Haven't drank like that in a while. Just needed some hair of the dog."

"That's a big hair," Lissa observed drily.

"It was a big dog," Gage grunted back at her. His slate grey eyes were unyielding beneath her ice-cold blue ones.

"Don't let it affect your judgment." Lissa looked away to resume her pacing. "We need to plan. Probably have to bring the Fangs in on it."

"Grant won't allow it," Gage said, shaking his head. "He won't risk starting a gang war by sending a group of Narcomancers into enemy territory."

"Those men can't be Breakers. None of them had their hammer tattoos. At best, they're tenants, nothing more."

"Tenants wouldn't have such a well-placed headquarters. It's too deep in Mills for them to be simply renting." Gage rubbed his chin as he thought. "You're right about them not being Breakers, but they must have permission to be operating there. Besides, I recognized a couple of the men who attacked us. They used to be friends of Tobias Malone. Perhaps he has returned to the city."

146

"Malone...I know that name, though I can't recall why." Lissa stopped pacing and looked at Gage to elaborate.

"He was my apprentice after you. I forced him to leave the city after I refused to teach him further."

"You forced him to leave? Why?" Lissa looked shocked at the revelation. Though it was shocking in truth. Most Narcomaners who dropped an apprentice wouldn't give much thought to what they did afterward. But Gage had made sure that Malone had left.

"We had a difference of opinion on how to employ our abilities."

"That's it? Those kinds of arguments happen all the time. They never end in one man chasing the other out of town." Her eyes were full of skepticism as they met his.

"He was obsessed with Blending. He believed he could balance the addictions and survive them." Gage took another big sip of whiskey. "He also believed we should kill Grant and take over the Fangs."

He could see the impact of his words on Lissa's face. Most gangs operated on those types of dynamics. The most powerful led and forced the others into line. But the Fangs were different. They followed Grant because he was intelligent and open-handed. Everyone played their part, and everyone got paid. Gage had recognized Malone's early ideas as the seeds of greed that would never stop growing if they found fertile ground.

"So, you ran him off to protect Grant?"

"Sort of." Gage shrugged his shoulders and set aside his now empty glass. "Malone was strong. Very strong. I knew if he found a place of power, even in a weaker gang, he would burn this city to ashes to feed his ambition. It seems that either his old lackeys have found a new leader, or he is back in the city."

"So, how do we handle him?"

"If he is around when we strike, then I will take care of him. He won't be able to resist fighting me on his own. He always believed he was better than me."

"So that would leave the rest of his men to me." She did not ask it; she knew it as a reality if

148

they found themselves in a similar situation as the previous night. He nodded to confirm it. He would have his hands full with Malone. Something occurred to him suddenly.

"Did you use cannin during the fight?" She nodded in confirmation.

"I Fogged the men on the roof to think we were still up there. And then I Fogged the men on the ground to think there were six of us." Gage rose from his seat and crossed the room to a small cabinet. He pulled a sheaf of papers out and brought them to the table in the center of the room.

"These are maps of all the slums, with each building in use marked with the color of the gang who controls it."

Lissa came to stand beside him as he spread the maps out. They depicted the whole city in intricate detail. Every building on every street was noted.

"How many men could you Fog at once?" Gage asked.

"Depends on what I'm trying to get them to do. A dozen at most." She looked at him questioningly.

"Chase you." Gage waved a hand at the maps. "I take on Malone, or if he's not there, as many as I can. You get the rest to chase you. Lead them to somewhere the Fangs can ambush and incapacitate them." Lissa looked at the map intently, considering the possibilities.

"The Barn?"

"Too far away," Gage said, shaking his head. "It would take at least an hour to get there on foot, even with coccin." They poured over the maps, searching for a building that might fit their needs. After several minutes, Lissa pointed to a particular building.

"Here." Gage looked at the building in question. It was just over the edge of the border that Mills shared with Tongs, just outside of Breakers territory. It was far enough to buy time and close enough that Lissa could be sure she wouldn't get caught by Malone's Blenders. Best of all, the building was currently abandoned. It would take a small bribe to the Stingers, the small gang that ruled Tongs, for them to use it.

"You'll still need help to lay the trap for them."

"Shouldn't be a problem." Lissa sounded confident. "Grant will let me take who I need. We can do this quickly and quietly. If it goes to plan, we can incapacitate them, call the constables, and be gone before anyone knows it was us. No threat of a gang war." Gage nodded at that. "We can set up a wagon there and take it back to help you grab your employer's goods as soon as the Blenders are taken care of."

It was a good plan. Well thought out, and there would be plenty of backup for Lissa. There would be none for Gage though.

"You're sure you can beat him? Malone?" Gage looked at her and saw the worry in her eyes. He nodded. Malone may be talented, but Gage had far more experience. Plus, he had his black leather bag, if it came to that.

They discussed a few more details, then Gage dismissed Lissa to contact members of the Fangs who she trusted to get the job done. She left quickly, her stride confident and purposeful. Gage was confident that their plan was solid. But a lot of it relied on chance and Gage had never much liked counting on chance.

Chapter 12

Dane stood across the street from Krayden's shop, trying to work up the courage to enter. He had spent all morning at the Barn with Storr and Tamar. They had spent several hours going over the many uses of baccin. He didn't have a pipe yet, so Storr had shown him how to roll loose baccin leaves into thin paper for cigarettes.

First, they had instructed him to get up onto one of the stilt-like wooden poles with a flat step on top. He expected they would then tell him to hop to the next one, but instead they had him balance on one foot for as long as he could. At first, he could barely maintain it for even a full minute, even with the baccin aiding his balance.

After several tries, he got the hang of it and could stand for almost half an hour before Storr gave the order for him to hop to the next post. Dane had missed by a lot and fallen hard to the floor. Luckily, he had taken Tamar's advice and drank a shot of liquor beforehand, so the fall didn't hurt. After several more tries, he had managed to land on the step atop the second post, but his excitement at managing the feat was undercut by Storr announcing that they were out of time and would have to wait until tomorrow to continue.

After taking Dane back to the house, Storr had told him that he and Tamar were needed for some business and would be gone the rest of the day and most of the night.

"Can I come?" Dane had asked. He had grown fond of the two men during their two days together.

"Sorry kid. This ain't apprentice work." Storr had ruffled his hair and told him to stay in the house until they returned. Tamar had offered a few words before they left.

"I know it is frustrating, yes?" His deliberate, Darashi accented speech had become familiar to Dane by now. "Soon enough, you will have work. But patience first." With that, the two men had walked out the door, and Dane was alone.

Being alone was difficult for Dane. He had nothing but his thoughts to dwell on and the predicament he faced made him anxious and fearful. He had three choices, he decided. He could flee the city now and try to find some quiet corner of the world to live a simple life. Once, that idea had appealed to him, but now, having tasted the power that he could have, Dane knew he could never walk away.

His second choice was to do nothing. To hope that Isar's threats were empty and that he could not truly hurt Dane. Dane couldn't convince himself that that was true. His mind said that Dane was a dopemage, and nothing should be a threat to him now. Dopemages were the most powerful people in the world. But he could not forget the look in Isar's eyes. Eyes that seemed old beyond belief. He also reminded himself of the strange things that had happened with Hal and Gun. There were perhaps other magics in the world of which he was ignorant. Magics stronger than Narcomancy. That thought chilled him.

His final option was to go through with the theft. This one was almost as terrifying as the second. Dane could think of no one who scared him more than Halfjaw. The scarred man was not just scary to look upon, but also in that he was one of the most talented dopemages in the world, according to Storr. Where Isar was an unknowable threat, Halfjaw was a known one. Dane could easily imagine the things Halfjaw could do to him. His stomach turned at the thought of it.

Ultimately, the decision he made was that he didn't have enough information to decide. Lissa had mentioned that Krayden knew about every dopemage in the city, and while Dane somehow doubted that Isar was a dopemage, he figured it wouldn't hurt to ask Krayden if he had heard of him. If he had, and if Isar was a dopemage, then at least Dane would know something about the man, even if it didn't make his choices much easier.

So, now he stood across from Krayden's shop, trying to force himself to enter. He knew he needed the knowledge, yet he feared the answers he might get. But it had to be done.

Dane straightened his new jacket; Storr had given it to him the night before. It was blood red and short, cut in a close-fitting style. It had the snarling wolf's head sigil of the Fangs stitched in black on the shoulder, which Storr had told him would offer him protection in some parts of the city. Though, he had also warned that the symbol could make him a target in certain areas.

Dane opened the shop door slowly, peering inside, even as he chastised himself for his shyness. Storr and Tamar had been teaching him that being a dopemage meant carrying himself like one. They had repeatedly stressed to him that he wasn't a farm boy anymore and should walk with pride. Dane had felt himself making progress in this arena, yet now alone and in unfamiliar territory, he hated how he shrank back inside himself.

Tally was standing at the counter as he entered. Her round face lit up as she saw him. Dane returned the smile, slowly, then forced himself to set his shoulders and approach.

"Dane, dear!" Tally exclaimed. "Back so soon! How is the training going?"

"It's okay." He couldn't keep the hesitancy out of his voice. Tally's enthusiastic nature was intimidating in its own way.

"Well, what can I do for you? Don't tell me you used up all your supplies already! Or are you looking for another lesson on Narcomancy?" The words tumbled out in a rush; Dane could hardly believe the woman found time to breathe with how fast she talked.

157

"Actually, I was hoping I could speak to Krayden?"

"Oh, dear, of course, of course!" She seemed slightly disappointed that he was not there to see her, but he put it out of his mind. As nice as she was, he had bigger concerns than Tally's feelings. Tally bustled to the back of the shop and knocked on the door. She poked her head in and Dane heard the quick, muffled exchange before she pulled back and waved for him to enter.

"Thanks, Tally." Dane was rewarded with a beaming smile as he left the shop and entered the back room. Krayden was bent over a stone table full of glassware. Some of the bottles were full of powders, some held samples of plants, and others were empty.

"Ah! Lissa's young friend!" The old man began shuffling some of the bottles around until they were gathered in the middle of the table, far away from the burning brazier that stood by the edge. He pointed to a stool. "Have a seat, my boy, have a seat."

Dane seated himself. He was unable to keep his eyes from wandering around the room. He

158

hadn't had much chance to examine it his last time here. The walls were covered in shelves loaded with substances, none of which he recognized. It was probably the strangest room he had ever been in.

"Hmm, so, what can I do for you...?" He hesitated, obviously having forgotten Dane's name.

"Dane, sir."

"Dane, hmm, yes. What can I do for you, Dane?"

"Well, sir, Lissa mentioned that you know all of the dopemages in the city —"

"Narcomancers, hmm. Call them Narcomancers, if you please. I'm a man of science and I like to refer to things by their proper titles. Besides, hm. That term, dopemage. It just sounds ridiculous and reductive."

"Yes, sir. Narcomancers. Lissa said you know all the Narcomancers in the city?" Dane felt a little awkward at the chastisement, but something about Krayden's simple, almost distracted air, as if he was constantly thinking of twelve different things, put him back at ease.

"Hmm, well yes, I do at that." He adjusted his spectacles and looked at Dane, truly focusing on him for the first time. "Now, you should know, if Lissa hasn't told you, in that regard, I am not a shopkeeper or provider of, hmm, well, extralegal, shall we say, goods. In this I am an employee of Mr. Grant. I see that you wear the Fangs sigil now, and so I can offer this service to you. But it is not something that is to be bandied about, hmm? If someone should ask where you came by the information you get from me, you must not disclose it, unless it is within gang circles."

"Yes, sir." Dane fought to remain confident under the old man's stare. "It is to satisfy my own curiosity. That's all, sir."

"Well, hmm, that's well enough. Just thought you ought to be informed." Krayden walked over to a cabinet and opened it, pulling out a large leather-bound book. There were many loose pages tucked in between the bound ones. "So, tell me, who is it you want to know about?"

"Well, it's a man I met yesterday. He was about fifty? He had short grey hair and a grey beard, all the same length. His eyes were really dark, and I couldn't place his accent. I believe his name is Isar."

Dane waited as Krayden perused the massive book. He flipped to different sections and scanned the pages faster than Dane thought possible. Dane could read, but slowly and with effort. Krayden seemed to read as if the pages spoke to him aloud. Dane found it fascinating.

"Hmmm, well, a Narcomancer of that age would be incredibly uncommon. And I would certainly be aware of them if any were in the city. However, hmm, the oldest currently in Alcaren is a man named Wist, and he is described as dark of hair with a scattering of grey. No beard and hazel eyes. And I have never heard of a man named Isar. Hmm, are you sure he is a Narcomancer?"

"No, sir. But he seemed dangerous. I just wanted to check, to be sure he wasn't."

"Well, young man, there are many dangerous people in this city who possess no magical gifts. Plenty of people skilled in arms and capable of despicable deeds, hmm. But, then again, you are a Narcomancer yourself, so you should have little to fear from such men."

"Yes, sir."

"Hmm, though I should also say this. It is possible this man has avoided my informants and has hidden his abilities. I do not think it is likely, but it is possible. Take care, hmm?"

"Yes, sir. Thank you, sir." The old man waved away the thanks and turned back to his table as Dane left. Tally was helping a customer as Dane exited the back room, so he left with a simple nod to her in thanks. She smiled in acknowledgment, and Dane left the store.

Dane was lost in thought as he walked through the busy streets of Arches. The sun was on its way down, dusk was coming fast. The information Krayden had provided hadn't really ruled anything out. In fact, the way he had seemed sure that Dane was safe from anyone who wasn't a dopemage, betrayed the fact that he didn't seem aware that there could be other magics out there.

An idea came to Dane suddenly. He was in Arches, probably near to the place that he was supposed to find Isar after completing his task. He had plenty of baccin cigarettes on him; Storr had made him practice rolling for a long time. He could nd the place where Isar could be located, stake it out and follow him if he left. Dane could observe him and see if he displayed any unusual abilities.

It was simple enough to ask a few people to point him in the direction of the Tilted Crown. He found it just as the sun was disappearing behind the Heights. An alley across from the entrance offered him an unobstructed view of the building. Now all he needed was for the man to appear.

Dane waited for a long time. It was well past sundown before he caught sight of his target. Isar exited the building and turned right, striding down the street with a quick, purposeful gait. Dane rose slowly and followed him. He kept as far back as he dared, keeping Isar in sight. The crowd had thinned, and it was no challenge to follow the man; in fact, more than once Dane told himself that there was no cover for him if Isar suddenly turned around. He pushed that thought away and resolved to continue, even as his nerves raged at him that this was foolishness.

Dane followed Isar for about half an hour, leaving Arches behind for one of the lesser slums. The light was worse here, night had fully fallen, and the streetlights were few and far between.

Suddenly, Isar turned down a side alley. He was almost two hundred feet ahead of Dane when he did so, and Dane rushed forward, worried about losing the man. He got up to the corner of the alley and peered in just in time to see Isar turn onto another street at the end of the alley. Dane started forward again and made it halfway down the alley when he was suddenly slammed into the side wall.

Dane felt his feet lift off the ground as his head and back were pressed against the rough wooden planking of the building. He looked down and felt his terror rise as he saw it was Isar who held him. The strange man held him up with one hand twisting Dane's collar tight against his throat. Anger burned in Isar's dark eyes.

Dane was embarrassed by his foolishness. He had followed a man he knew nothing about, with no experience in stalking. He had smoked a couple of baccin cigarettes but hadn't thought to take any alcohol or coccin. He was helpless.

"Did you really think I wouldn't notice you following me? I have lived far longer than you can imagine and seen things you would never believe. You cannot fathom what I am capable of." Dane tried to reply, but Isar twisted his collar further, pushing it into his throat so he couldn't speak. "Luckily for you, I need someone to do this task, and you are best positioned for it. So, I will refrain from disposing of you…for now."

Isar lowered Dane so his feet touched the ground. He loomed over Dane. Had he gotten taller? Were his ears now pointed? He suddenly seemed alien in ways that Dane could not describe, and the full weight of his folly struck him like a blow. Isar tossed him to the ground like a child might toss a doll, and with the same careless force.

Dane felt the breath forced from his lungs as his back hit the ground. He wanted to get up and flee. He wanted to find some hole and hide from the world. Somehow, he knew that would not save him from this man. This creature.

"You will do as I have ordered. Or I will see you meet a swift and painful end." Isar looked down at him with disgust in his eyes. "Tonight, will be your best opportunity. Don't waste it." With that, Isar turned and strode from the alley.

Dane lay dazed where he had been tossed. His breath was returning, but his body was blooming with fresh bruises. It was difficult to admit, but it seemed his decision had been made for him.

Chapter 13

Lissa crouched by the mouth of an alley, looking at the back of the warehouse, opposite from where they had been caught the night before. Halfjaw stood behind her, pressed tightly to the side of the building. It was almost midnight, and the light of the two moons was obscured by heavy clouds. The few streetlamps offered little light in this area of Mills.

They had seen only a couple of guards since they had started watching. Everything seemed the same as the night before, except tonight, Lissa and Halfjaw hadn't been foolish enough to let themselves be seen. There were a number of large windows on the ground floor that would provide an excellent entryway for them. After that, they would have to hope they had planned for any eventualities.

Lissa could feel the coccin in her system; it made her jittery and restless. She wasn't used to using coccin much. She preferred cannin and baccin. Deception and stealth. But tonight, she would need to fight. She had also smoked a large amount of cannin and had a wad of chew in her lip. The mixture of the three drugs was difficult to balance and she knew she wouldn't be able to handle alcohol on top of them. She didn't have as much practice at Blending as Halfjaw did.

She was just thinking they should move in soon, when Halfjaw tapped her shoulder. She looked back at him, and he nodded once. It was time. She moved first, creeping across the narrow street and up against the warehouse wall, just below one of the windows. Halfjaw followed behind after waiting to see if her approach had been noticed. It hadn't.

Lissa stood slowly, pulling her belt knife and using it to quietly slip the simple latch on the window. It opened outward on quiet hinges. The inside was dark, a few lanterns burned softly at the other end, but no one seemed to be about. She slipped over the edge of the window easily and dropped quietly to the floor. Halfjaw followed quickly; he wasn't quite as quiet as she was, but he was still impressively soft-footed.

With them both inside, they moved toward the part of the warehouse where Halfjaw had seen the boxes when he had spied before. Their eyes had adjusted to the near darkness when they reached the intended area. The boxes were there and were recognizable by the quality compared to those around them. The ones on top had obviously been opened; likely all of them had been. She was just thinking they might not need the plan after all. Then, lights began to appear above them.

Four large lanterns came to life on the walkway that ran around the outer wall. Six smaller ones bloomed into existence in a semicircle around them on the ground floor. Footsteps sounded on the walkway as the men up there began to move, lighting more lanterns until the whole room was decently lit. Six men stood around Lissa and Halfjaw, pinning them against the wall. Four more men stood on the walkways. One of the men on the ground floor was Bull; he leered at them like a wolf who had managed to tree his prey.

One more man was there, walking down the steps from the walkways to the ground. He was tall and thin; his cheeks were sunken, and his skin was as pale as milk. But his brown eyes were bright and clever. She guessed this was Malone. She glanced at Halfjaw, the glare he had fixed on the man confirmed her suspicions. Hopefully,

Halfjaw knew the man as well as he thought he did.

Malone approached, stepping between the men fencing Lissa and Halfjaw in. His clothes were well worn, but finely made. He wore a long coat like Halfjaw's but made of better leather and less beaten up.

"Harlon Gage." Malone sneered the name, his satisfaction at the situation plain. "So good to see my old teacher again." He peered intently at Halfjaw, not taking any notice of Lissa. "I had heard about your…injury, but I didn't expect this. You were never a handsome man, but now?" He made a noise of disgust. "You're just plain hideous!" Lissa wasn't sure if he was trying to goad Halfjaw, but if he was, she knew it was the wrong strategy. Halfjaw was not a vain man.

"I should've killed you all those years ago." There was no heat in Halfjaw's voice, just resignation. His grey eyes were hard though; he was ready for the fight. The four men on the walkways threw themselves over the railings, dropping heavily to the floor. They staggered and stumbled to their feet, moving forward to close the holes in the circle around Lissa and Halfjaw.

"But you didn't. And now, I am going to kill you. And then everyone will know that I am the best Narcomancer in this city. Not you! Me!" Malone's voice grew louder with every word, a mad light shone in his eyes. This man was not entirely sane. Maybe Halfjaw's plan would work.

Halfjaw nodded to Malone, not looking at Lissa. He stepped forward, pulling a glass vial of coccin from his jacket.

"The old way then?" This was it, the most critical moment, the whole of the plan hinged on it. Malone stared at Halfjaw, eyes burning with hate. He nodded.

"The old way."

The two men threw themselves at each other in a blur of violence. Lissa sprang clear and turned toward the ten men blocking her escape. Three of them, including Bull, were advancing on her. She surprised them by sprinting straight at them. She could see the shock on their faces as she flew at them; they had not expected her to attack. And she didn't. As soon as she was within striking distance, she threw herself under the oncoming blows, rolling across the floor and clear of the circle.

Lissa could hear the sounds of Halfjaw's fight, and it was difficult to leave him, but she knew she had to. She pushed her thoughts outward, a strong mental command.

Follow me, follow me. Catch me, catch me.

She saw the command wash over them and immediately turned to the other end of the warehouse, racing for the door. She pulled a vial of coccin from her jacket; she hadn't bothered changing into dark clothes tonight. She wanted to be seen.

Lissa pulled the cork from the vial, held it to her nostril, and snorted the whole thing. Her nose burned and her eyes watered, but her mind exploded in pleasure and energy. She pushed the pleasure of the drug that threatened to drown her and held it back. The energy, she let flood her limbs, obeying the urge to move. She could hear the ringing footsteps crashing across the floor behind her as she crashed through the door. She was ten steps past it before realizing that she hadn't even bothered to open it.

She raced around the corner of the building, turning towards Tongs. She fled through the warren of narrow streets and side alleys. The drugs sang in her blood, urging her to move faster and faster. This was what it meant to be a Narcomancer. To touch power no one else could imagine. But also, to constantly have to hold back, never able to give in to your base impulses lest the addictions overcome you. More than once, she had to force herself to slow down and glance back, to make sure her pursuers stayed within reach.

Twice Lissa flung mental commands back at them, enticing them with the chance of catching and killing her. It was a subtle thing. Small impressions that stoked their anger and urged them on. She convinced their minds that they were closing in, that she was tiring, that she had no place to go. All the while she stayed safely ahead of them, her strength unflagging and her course chosen deliberately.

She reached the warehouse they had chosen, flinging the doors wide, not bothering to close them behind her. She sprinted for the far wall as she heard the heavy steps of the men flooding into the building. She reached the back wall and turned, just in time to see the trap snap shut. There were enough lanterns lit to see by, so she had a clear view as the weighted nets were thrown down from the upper floor.

Six of the men were caught easily. The nets fell on them, wrapping around their limbs and twisting them up so that they could not keep their feet in their inebriated state.

Fang members leaped from the shadows at the edges of the warehouse. Some went to ensure the containment of the men in the nets. Others ganged up and pulled down two more men as they tried to reach Lissa. That left two more, one of them Bull, charging toward Lissa, seemingly oblivious to their fellows' predicament.

The man, whose name she didn't know stepped in what looked like a harmless coil of rope, and his leg was immediately seized by the ankle, the snare launching him into the air to hang upside down. She knew that snare; it was Tamar's work.

Bull was bearing down on her now, and Lissa was ready for him. She still smarted over how he had thrown the table at her a few days ago. She was still running high on coccin, so much that even with Bull Blending coccin and alcohol, he seemed sluggish and weak by comparison. She sidestepped each of his heavy, wild swings, bending aside as easily as a willow switch.

Bull tried to pin her up against the wall, but she was too nimble, and he was too drunk to match her speed and coordination. That was the downside to Blending. Coccin gave a Narcomancer speed and strength, but alcohol robbed them of the coordination to use those skills well unless they were well practiced.

Soon enough, Lissa was striking back. For each blow she dodged, she struck back twice. They were little things, a jab here, a kick there. But they would add up. She could tell he was slowing and after a particularly strong kick, she saw him wince. His alcohol was wearing off. He knew it too. He backed off, retreating so he stood in the open area of the warehouse floor, the second-floor balcony loomed over him.

Lissa thought about following him and preventing him from drinking from the flask he was now pulling out of his jacket. His eyes were angry as he raised it quickly to his lips, his throat moved as he swallowed.

And then the large smith's anvil dropped from above, crushing him into the floorboards.

Lissa had thought it a ridiculous suggestion when Storr had mentioned it. He had gotten the two-hundred-pound iron anvil from a smithy that went out of business. He originally thought he might take up blacksmithing as a hobby but found he had no talent for it. Lissa was not surprised, as he had talent for little aside from Narcomancy and gambling.

Looking down at the splintered floor and shattered body of her opponent, she had to admit that the strategy was effective, if a bit underhanded. Then again, they had intended to fight her ten to one.

"What do you think?" Storr asked, appearing next to her after leaping from the second floor.

"I think Grant is gonna be pissed about having to pay to fix that floor."

"Yeah, yeah. But it worked, huh?" Storr's smile was ear to ear.

"All the others still alive?" Lissa was glad Bull was dead, but she couldn't revel in violence the way that Storr, and many of the others, did. It was a thing that needed to be done. That didn't mean she had to take joy in it.

"Yeah, they're all still kicking. We've got them secured well enough, though."

The rush of the coccin was beginning to wear off, and she knew she would be useless once it did. There were still things to do tonight.

"Good. Check if any of them are Breakers. We can ransom them back to the gang if they are." Lissa lit a fresh cigarette and took a long drag. It was pleasant to feel the baccin run through her, refreshing her senses. "Then get the wagon. We need to get back to Halfjaw and get him out of there by dawn."

Storr rushed off to do as she had told him. Lissa hoped they would be in time to help Halfjaw if he needed it.

Chapter 14

Gage and Malone leapt at each other at the same time. His plan had worked, this part anyway. Lissa was on her own now, and hopefully, her part would go smoothly. He could tell from the first blow that both he and Malone were Blending. Alcohol, coccin, and baccin; all used in concert by experts in the art. Malone had been inexperienced when Gage had exiled him, but it was clear he had been trained well since then.

Malone didn't fight like a grappler, or like a wild man. He fought with precise strikes and powerful blows. It was a difficult thing to do while drunk and high, but with practice and a well cultivated tolerance, it was possible. They fought without thought for self-defense or care of the things around them. Crates were smashed, walls were dented, and windows were shattered.

It wasn't until they broke apart, each retreating a dozen steps to refuel themselves, that Gage realized Lissa had succeeded in drawing away the rest of Malone's goons. That was good, not just for her, but for himself. He doubted that

Malone would hold to the old ways if he began to lose. At least now, Gage could be sure he would win or lose on his own. Unless Lissa's part failed, that is. He pushed that thought away. She wouldn't fail.

"You haven't changed much." Malone sucked down his flask of liquor and pulled a vial of coccin out. "Aside from that scar and the dent in your face." Gage said nothing but saw to his own needs. He emptied his flask and took a fresh snort of coccin. He lit a cigarette and took several long drags. "How did that happen anyway? Someone finally got the better of you?"

"Nobody gets the better of me," Gage grunted out the response. He was angry at himself for even answering but his pride wouldn't let this man think he could be beaten. That was part of the fight, believing you would win.

"I did," Malone pulled a white hartshorn pipe from his jacket, lit the bowl and raised it to his sneering lips. He took a pull, his bright eyes laughing. Gage felt the growl rise in his throat, but bit it back. He knew that Malone was behind the robbery, but him holding Gage's pipe was a visceral reminder of that night. Of Faron's death.

He flicked the rest of his cigarette aside. He was ready.

"You can have it back if you beat me," Malone placed the pipe on top of one of the crates that belonged to Gage's employer. "But you won't!"

Malone flung himself at Gage again, and the fight resumed at its previous breakneck pace. It was difficult to process each moment of it. Blows came in rushes, never leaving a mark. They were an even match for each other, a fact that rankled Gage's pride. He did not like to think about the fact that he was getting old. Not for a normal person, perhaps. But for a Narcomancer, thirty-five was a ripe age.

More damage was done to the warehouses around them. Punches that missed left holes in the walls or emptied windows of their glass. Kicks left holes and dents in the floorboards. Gage noticed none of it, all he saw was the mad visage of Malone, eyes blazing as they crashed against each other again and again.

They broke apart again, both of them panting a bit at the exertion of the fight. Gage pulled out the second of the three flasks he carried and emptied it into his mouth. He had two more vials of coccin as well; it was probably all he could take without overdosing. Perhaps it was enough. Perhaps this was the time he overdid it, and his body failed him. He forced his mind away from those doubts.

"What interest do you have in my employer's goods?" The thought occurred to him suddenly as he lit another cigarette. All the things he had seen in the few boxes he had saved had no interest to a man like Malone.

"Interest?" Malone snorted. "None save what *my* employer pays me to have. I have no interest in the squabbling of rich merchants. I took this job because I was promised a shot at you. And here we are." Malone had emptied another flask and another vial. He was ready again. Gage flicked his cigarette away again, the spark at its end glowing as it vanished into the shadows.

The fight resumed at its reckless, breakneck pace. Gage could feel himself becoming wilder, less controlled as the drugs dragged him deeper into intoxication. He was stronger and faster than he had been in a long time, but he was also far drunker. It was harder to control his blows and harder to care when they struck something other than Malone. His emotions were losing cohesion as well. His anger was outgrowing his ability to control it.

That control was one of the things that made Gage the feared and respected Narcomancer that he was. When other men gave in to their rising emotions when Raging, Gage kept himself under control. It allowed him to outthink his opponents. And it was one of the reasons he had exiled Malone.

Malone never kept himself in check. His emotions were fierce and untamed, as was his ambition. Soon after Gage had taken him as an apprentice, Malone had started saying that Grant had no right to lead the gang. He advocated for Gage taking control. For the Fangs being run the way the other gangs were. Gage had no such ambitions, however, and he had told Malone to never mention it again. But Malone could not contain himself. Gage saw the chaos he could cause as an unleashed Narcomancer and so had refused to train him further, and after seeing how Malone cursed at him and swore vengeance, Gage had forced him to leave the city.

The fight was losing all cohesion now, both men devolving into flailing, brawlers rather than trained fighters. They were each sweating heavily, the stink of it filling the air to Gage's enhanced sense of smell. They broke apart again, each stumbling back from the other.

Gage pulled out another vial and snorted it without thinking. It was difficult to keep his head now. He had one vial left, one flask, and two cigarettes. He lit the first of the cigarettes, sucking down the smoke, but it wasn't enough to clear his head entirely. It would have to do. Malone had also lit a cigarette and was snorting a fresh vial.

"You should just give up, Halfjaw." He sneered the epithet, and Gage had to force down the rage that welled inside him. He knew people called him that and tried to act as if he did not care. But he did. He cared deeply. But some things couldn't be helped.

Malone held his jacket open fully for the first time, allowing Gage to see the four fresh flasks it held. He could see several more vials of coccin as well. Gage knew then that Malone would happily overdose before allowing himself to lose.

"You're a fool," Gage grunted as he tossed aside the finished cigarette and lit his last one. He pulled out his final flask and unscrewed the lid. He thought about the black leather sack tucked into the back of his belt. He didn't want to do this. It was risky, so risky. But as he often told himself, some things couldn't be helped.

As Malone tipped his head back and gulped at his flask, Gage sprang forward. He saw the shock in Malone's eyes as Gage threw his flask's contents, three ounces of pure grain liquor, straight into Malone's face. Malone dropped his empty flask and threw his hands out to push Gage away, but Gage got in close enough to press the lit end of his cigarette to the liquor-soaked skin of Malone's face.

The alcohol lit up immediately. Malone's whole face was engulfed in flame. Gage pulled the leather sack from his belt. Good thick, Marthen leather. Very hard to burn.

The flames caused no damage to Malone, but they blinded him.

Gage ducked around a wild blow, sweeping behind Malone as he swatted at the fire covering his face. The flames wouldn't hurt him. His skin couldn't be pierced or burnt; his bones couldn't be broken, his throat couldn't be crushed.

But he still needed to breathe.

Gage took the edges of the sack in both hands and swung it down over Malone's head. He pulled it tight against Malone's face, pulling the drawstrings so the bag was sealed fully around the madman's neck. Gage wrapped the strings once, twice, three times around his fists to ensure his grip. He slipped his leg between Malone's and pressed his weight against the other man's back. Gage rode him to the floor, knee pressed into the small of Malone's back.

Malone thrashed and flailed, panic setting in as he realized what Gage was doing. Gage fought to keep his position atop the struggling man. It was an exhausting effort, but Gage was a determined man.

After what felt like an eternity, the struggles lessened. It became easier and easier to hold Malone down. His hands clawed at the black leather, but they had no chance of even scoring the high-quality material. Eventually, the struggles ceased altogether. Gage held him down for several minutes after that, not willing to take the risk that Malone was faking.

Finally, Gage let himself roll off the corpse of Tobias Malone. He lay there, drunk and high, exhausted and weak. He hoped desperately that Lissa had succeeded in her part of the plan. Not just because he wanted her to be well, but because if one of them came back, he was in no condition to fight further. Between the drinking and the coccin, he could barely pull himself into a sitting position, let alone stand.

He reached under Malone's body, fishing around until he found the pocket where he kept his cigarettes. He was about to put one to his lips, when he remembered the pipe. He could see it, sitting atop a crate a couple dozen feet away. The distance seemed insurmountably far, but his pride had been pricked by Malone's use of his favorite pipe. He dragged himself to his feet and tottered over to the crate.

Gage grabbed the pipe, holding it up to the light. It had a small chip in the bowl which must have happened the night of the robbery. But it was still his. He found the pouch he kept his tobacco in, stuffed a pinch into the bowl, and lit it. He slumped against the crates, puffing on the stem and feeling whole despite his exhaustion.

The sound of horses outside roused him before he could pass out.

Well, here it is. The moment of truth. That was either the wagon that Lissa was supposed to bring, or reinforcements for Malone. He thought about trying to stand; if this was the end, he'd rather face it on his feet, but his body would not cooperate.

Relief flooded Gage's body when Lissa rushed through the doorway. She slowed as she came upon the scene. He could see the dismay in her eyes when she caught sight of the face-down body with a bag over its head. He saw also the relief in her when she saw him propped up against the crates, pipe in his mouth.

"So," she said as she approached. "You got your pipe back."

Gage nodded to her. Even speaking was almost beyond him at this point. He jabbed his tongue into the soft spot where his jawbone used to be. The pain flared as usual. The alcohol had worn off, but his body was still processing it. He noticed Lissa staring at Malone's body.

"Never thought about smothering before. Seems kind of obvious now." She walked over to it, bent down, and removed the sack. She walked back over to Gage and dropped it in his lap. "Wouldn't do for this strategy to become common knowledge." Gage nodded again.

"H-how do we say he died?" Gage grunted. Malone's body was unmarked. It would be noticed that there were no wounds. Lissa just shrugged.

"Let them wonder about the great and mysterious powers of Harlon 'Halfjaw' Gage." She smiled at him, and he found he did not mind his nickname so much when she said it. She pulled him to his feet, letting him lean against her. She took the pipe from his mouth and examined it.

"It's a little beat up since I gave it to you." He could do nothing more than nod at that. He was so tired. She seemed aware of it, for she forced her shoulder up under his arm and began leading him toward the door. "We'll have Storr and Tamar load up the wagon, then we'll get you to bed." He barely had the presence of mind to nod at that. His eyes were heavy, and his feet were leaden. He barely noticed Storr and Tamar taking him and helping him into the wagon. He was asleep before the first box was loaded into the bed.

Chapter 15

Dane circled the block for the third time, staring at the impressive stone building that contained Halfjaw's apartment. Lissa had shown it to him when she took him to Krayden's. She had pointed it out as an example of how well a dopemage could do if they were smart and skilled. Dane couldn't imagine living in such a nice place. An entire apartment all to himself, all his own.

But, to make it a reality, he would have to do as Isar said. Otherwise, he was sure he'd be dead within a week, if that.

Dane considered the building from all angles. The third floor was the highest, with a flat stone roof ringed by a low ledge. If he could get up there, he might be able to lower himself to one of the windows of the apartment. But there was no way up that he could see.

He considered trying to bluff his way inside the building, maybe convince someone that he had a package to drop off for Halfjaw. But he doubted the man would have left a key with someone else. Which would mean even if he got inside, he would have to slip the lock. All he had was his belt knife, and while he could probably make it work, it would leave notches that Halfjaw would undoubtedly notice.

He began to inspect the surrounding buildings. The front of the apartment building faced the wide street. One side faced a smaller side street and the other two faced buildings separated by narrow alleys. One of those buildings was a one-story blacksmith's shop. No help there. The other one, though…

It was three stories, just like the apartment building. If he could find a way up to that roof, he could make that leap, particularly if he used some of his coccin.

Storr had warned him not to try the drug without him there. He had warned Dane that a small amount would be a lot for him, as he had no tolerance built up. It would limit how much he could use the power until he amassed a familiarity with it. But, if he took just a tiny bit, it should be enough to boost him across the ten-foot gap.

Dane circled around to inspect the target building. It was stone as well, but older than

Halfjaw's building. The lines of mortar were worn low; he might be able to slip his fingers in there and pull himself up. But that would be slow, arduous work.

When he reached the back of the building, he found what he needed. The chimney was old and poorly maintained. The bricks had spaces between them large enough to fit the tip of his boot. With baccin to enhance his sense of touch and balance, he should be able to make the climb.

Dane searched his jacket until he found the pouch of chewing baccin that Storr had given him for training. He had taught Dane how to pack it into his lip, insisting it was better for use when active than the smoking baccin.

He took a pinch of the loose, pungent chew, pulled his front lip out, and stuffed the little ball between his front lip and gums. He had seen Storr simply pop the chew into his mouth and force it down with his tongue, but when Dane had tried that method, the chew had broken apart, spilling over his tongue and making him vomit. Storr and Tamar had found that quite amusing.

Dane was about to set his hands to the worn bricks, when he remembered how unprepared he had been for his confrontation with Isar. He had not thought about the consequences when he decided to tail the strange man and had suffered for it.

He pulled his flask out and took a swig, enough to protect him if he fell, but not so much that it would disorient him as he climbed. Then, after a brief consideration, took out the small vial of coccin he had in his pouch. He tapped a small amount onto the back of his hand, a tiny fraction of what was in the vial. He hesitated as he raised his hand to his nose, apprehension rose in him, but so did a small measure of excitement. This was the substance most people talked about when they told stories of dopemages. That this little white powder gave men the strength of gods. And now Dane was going to taste that power.

He pressed the back of his hand to his face and snorted. The powder burned as it traveled up his nostril. The effect was instantaneous. His mind rushed with thought after thought, faster than he could consider them. His blood thrummed with power. It urged him to run, to jump, to fight. And he so badly wanted to do as it bid him.

Storr had warned of this, however. He was able, after a moment of nearly surrendering to it, to pull himself back and fight down the feelings it manifested.

Dane shook his head, and resolutely set himself to his task. He set his fingers to the bricks above his head. He found purchase for them, digging his fingers into the ruts between the bricks, feeling every bit of the rough surface. He pulled himself up, set his boot tips into similar ruts about a foot off the ground.

The climb was agonizingly slow. He had to find adequate holds for not just his fingers, but also for where his feet would need to follow. By the time he reached the top, even with the added strength of coccin, his shoulders burned, and his ankles ached.

Dane let his body slump as he pulled himself onto the roof. He lay there panting for a time, staring up at the overcast night sky. The moons' light was barely visible through the clouds. He guessed that it was almost midnight now. Isar had warned him that he had until dawn.

After his aches began to fade, Dane pushed himself to his feet, swaying slightly. He pulled the wad of chew out of his lip and replaced it with a fresh one.   His senses sharpened, and his mind cleared a bit. After a moment of consideration, he took the vial out and snorted another small line of coccin. He was better prepared for the rush this time and withstood it easier.

He walked to the edge of the roof and surveyed the gap between this building and Halfjaw's. As he had guessed, it was about a ten-foot leap. With the energy flowing through him, he knew that he could make it.

Dane backed up a few steps, gauging the speed he would need to generate to make it. After reminding himself that he had alcohol to protect him if he missed, he hardened his resolve and ran. As his foot hit the lip of the roof, he threw all his strength into the leap.

Dane had grossly misjudged the strength that coccin lent a man. He soared over the gap, clearing it easily. Instead of landing on the edge of the other roof, he crossed almost an additional ten feet, tumbling to the roof in shock.

He was unhurt, thanks to the alcohol, but he was stunned by the magnitude of what he had just done. He had leapt over twenty feet with almost no running start. It was incredible. He wondered instantly, if that little coccin could give him such strength. How much would he be able to muster when he learned to use it well? With that kind of power, he might be able to overcome Isar.

Dane pulled his thoughts back from that line of thinking. Scolding himself for his eagerness to abandon logic. Even if someday he managed that level of power, it would not be soon. Storr and Tamar had told him again and again that it would take years to acquire the kind of skills he would need to consider himself a full Narcomancer.

His problems were for today and they must be dealt with now. He could not count on this to save him.

Dane moved closer to the corner of the roof above Halfjaw's apartment. He looked down, searching for potential hand and footholds. But unlike the other building, this one was in excellent repair. The stones had no weakened mortar, no notches or ridges to cling to. That was probably why Halfjaw had chosen this place to live.

The only chance Dane saw was the ledge that protruded from underneath the window. It was wide enough for one foot, maybe not even that much. If he positioned his fall correctly, he could land with both feet sideways, and with the enhanced balance that baccin offered, he might be able to not fall off. It was not an encouraging prospect.

Knowing he would need all the help he could get, Dane replaced his chew again, then lit a cigarette and smoked it down to the butt. After some thought, he lit another and smoked that down too. Then he replaced his chew again. Confident he had taken all the baccin he could without making himself sick, he leaned over the edge and planned his fall.

When he was ready, he checked the sky. He could see no stars, but by the faint light of the moons, he guessed it was just past midnight now. He could not afford to wait much longer.

He took another small swig of the grain liquor in his flask and readied himself. It was no easy thing to let himself fall from the top of a building. He worked up the nerve after reminding himself that the fall would not hurt him. He levered himself over the edge and hung by his hands. He looked down, trying to judge the correct line. When he thought he had it lined up correctly, he let go.

Dane's feet hit the ledge faster than he anticipated. Luckily, his weight was positioned so he fell first against the building before tipping toward the empty air. It gave him just enough time to grab the underside of the top of the window. His fingers barely managed to find a grip, but it was enough.

He stood there, shakily balanced, trying to calm his breathing. After a moment, the threat of danger vanished, and the thrill of the accomplishment rushed through him. He grinned to the night sky, unable to contain his pleasure at this feat. A week ago, he had been a poor farm boy, son of a miserable man, doomed to the fate of working a field for the rest of his life. Now he ran across rooftops and danced on window ledges. He was a dopemage.

After a moment, Dane forced his attention back to his task. He studied the window frame and found where the latch at the bottom held it shut. There was just enough room for his knife blade.

After a few careful tries, he managed to catch the latch and flip it. He pushed the glass panes inward and slipped into the room as quietly as he could.

He found himself in a sparsely furnished sitting room. Two decent chairs and a plain wooden table. A few cabinets and a simple kitchen. He searched the cabinets but found nothing that could be what he was looking for.

He tried one of the other two rooms; it was the bedroom. Dane carefully looked through the wardrobe, under the bed, and even in the small privy chamber. Nothing.

Dane looked into the third room, finding himself in a study. A simple desk and chair were in one corner, shelves filled with books lined the walls. Dane had never had much use for books, but he still found the sight impressive. There was a closet in this room, and when he checked it, he found what he was looking for.

Three wooden crates were buried under an assortment of clutter, but they were definitely the ones he sought. He carefully put the clutter aside, making sure to take note of what had been on top and what had been crammed into the sides.

Dane was shocked by the number of papers he found in the crates. Hundreds, if not thousands, of pages were packed into the boxes. It would take him hours to sort through this. He forced himself not to panic. He didn't need to read all of it, he just needed to search for a letter to a man named Waylan that spoke of Old Marth. He would just need to scan each page for those words.

Even with those specific parameters, the process was slow and irritating. After at least an hour, his efforts were rewarded. The top of the page was addressed to a Master Waylan. He could have just taken it and left, but he wanted to be sure it was the right one. A small part of him also wanted to see what about this information was so valuable to Isar. So, he smoothed the page out and read.

Master Waylan,

I believe our efforts have finally yielded the results you desired. After traveling up to the headwaters of the Purath River, I finally located the ruins of Old Marth. It is truly desolate. However, after a few days of searching the surrounding area, we found a trail. It led up into the higher parts of the mountains. The going was difficult, but we found what we sought at the end. A tribe of people who have not had contact with the rest of the world since the land was split. They refused to talk with me until I invoked my father's name, as you suggested.

They greeted me warmly then. My companions and I were feasted and celebrated as the sons of heroes. Their princess herself came and offered us their hospitality for as long as we desired. She was beautiful and kind, with a glowing blue gem bound by silver on her brow.

I have found it, sir. And I am certain it is safe beyond any intervention less than the Nine themselves.

Your servant and friend always,

Orys Tor

Dane could make little sense of the meaning behind these words. But it didn't matter. He had the letter, and he would deliver it as ordered.

Dane returned to the window he had entered through and perched himself on the ledge outside it. He pulled the window closed and used his knife to flip the latch back. It didn't click into place, but it was close enough that Halfjaw likely wouldn't notice it had been undone.

He let himself drop to the ground, trusting the alcohol to leave him unhurt. After that he made his way across Arches, back to the Tilted Crown, where he knew he would find Isar waiting. Even now, with a couple of hours until dawn, he was sure the man would be ready for him.

He entered the common room of the inn, only a few lanterns were lit, and the hearth fire burned low, leaving the room mostly in shadow. He was about to approach the man at the bar, when he noticed someone sitting at one of the tables near the hearth. Dane's eyes met Isar's and, even now that he had accomplished his task, he felt himself quiver under that stare.

Dane walked over and seated himself across from Isar. The man eyed him as if he were anyone else. No sign of eagerness or anger on his face.

"Well?"

Dane slid the folded paper across the table wordlessly. Isar picked it up, unfolded it, and read it. One corner of his mouth turned up in a small smile.

"You've done well. Your debt is paid." Dane nodded at that and began to rise. "However…" Dane paused at that, turning his gaze back to the strange man. Isar indicated the seat, and Dane lowered himself back down into it.

"I will be leaving for a while, but when I return, I could use someone as talented as you." Isar's dark eyes seemed to bore into Dane. "Barely a week as a Narcomancer, and you managed to steal from one of the most feared men on all of Kalkis. I can teach you things, things that will lead you to power far greater than that of a simple Narcomancer."

Dane was stunned by these words. A simple Narcomancer? Narcomancers were the most powerful people in the world. When he vocalized this, Isar chuckled.

"Most powerful in *this* world, perhaps. But there are other worlds out there. And there are more powers to be explored. Things that do not require the kinds of sacrifices that Narcomancy demands. When I return, and it may be quite some time before I do, I will make this offer again." He raised his hand when Dane opened his mouth. "Do not answer now. Think about it. Think of the limitations these powers of yours place on you. And when I return, when you have had a few years to consider how short the life of Narcomancer truly is, then I will have your answer."

"If you have this kind of power, why did you need me to steal the letter? Why not do it yourself?" Isar leaned forward, fixing his dark eyes on him intently.

"There are certain laws, rules that govern the universe. One of these prohibits me from taking certain actions. That is all you need to know." Dane suddenly realized something. Lissa and Halfjaw had not been able to find any sign of who had been behind the men that robbed Halfjaw.

"You arranged the robbery, didn't you? That's how you knew that the letter was in the boxes that Halfjaw had." Isar gave a slight nod, then turned his attention to the letter in his hand.

Sensing that he was dismissed, Dane fled the inn. The things Isar had said were madness. Other worlds? It made no sense. But doubts still crept into Dane's mind. He had done things Dane could not understand. He suddenly realized how tired he was. He had been up all day and night, dealing with lies and other things that were beyond him. He wanted to just curl up on his pallet at the house and rest.

So, he put these insane things from his mind, set his feet toward Hollows, and left the strange man behind.

For now.

Epilogue

Lissa hopped down from the wagon as it rumbled to a stop outside of Halfjaw's building. The sun was beginning to peek over the eastern horizon. She felt stiff and tired, though she was in much better shape than Halfjaw. He managed to stumble down from his seat without falling, but his skin was paler than usual, and his eyes were sunken. He walked into the building, eager to get the other boxes he had saved from the robbery. Tamar went to help him, but Storr stayed atop the driver's bench of the wagon, holding the reins for the horses.

"How is Dane doing?" Lissa asked. She realized she had given little thought to her apprentice since dumping on Storr and Tamar.

"Oh, the kid's doing well," Storr said easily. "He's strong, Lissa. Really strong. We tested him in the usual ways. Took nearly ten minutes for Tamar and me to beat his alcohol reserves down. He held his baccin for nearly an hour, balanced on a post on one foot. Grant's gonna be happy with him."

"I'll admit, I'm a bit surprised to hear that. He seemed so meek and nervous."

"Oh, he's those things too. But I think he'll come around. He was disappointed when we left him behind last night." That was good. It was encouraging that the boy was showing signs of some eagerness for his new life. She wasn't sure if he would take to it. Grant would indeed be pleased.

"So," Storr looked at her with a grin. "You think we'll get a reward from this fancy employer of Halfjaw's?"

"He seemed to think so." Lissa herself doubted it. She knew too many of those rich merchant types to believe they'd show any genuine appreciation for their help. "At the very least, Halfjaw owes us one. And that's no small thing."

"That's true enough." She could see a hint of disappointment in his face, despite the words. Money meant more than favors to men like Storr.

Halfjaw and Tamar returned, carrying three small crates. She was amazed that Halfjaw could still move at all, let alone carry a crate down two sets of steps. The two men added their loads to the wagon's cargo. Halfjaw stepped up to the front of the wagon and held out his hand to Storr.

"You and Tamar go back to Hollows. Lissa and I will take the wagon from here." Storr looked like he would object, but instead, he shut his mouth and hopped down, handing the reins to Halfjaw. Halfjaw managed to haul himself up onto the bench, swaying slightly. Lissa hopped up beside him.

"You sure you're good to do this? You look half dead." Halfjaw looked at her, and a small smile turned up the corner of his mouth.

"Only half?"

"I was being generous." She couldn't help smiling back. It was the first time she had seen Halfjaw smile since this whole thing had started.

"Of course." Halfjaw snapped the reins and the horses moved. He guided them toward the main road that led up to the gates to the Heights. "You ready to meet the boss?"

"What's he like?"

"He's...different. A small man, kind, but there's something about him. He's like no one I've ever met. It's tough to explain, but you'll see soon enough. I've only met him once, but it was a memorable experience."

Gage guided the wagon into the empty courtyard of a large manor house. It was more ornate than any building he had ever been inside, though it was fairly tame by the standards of the Heights. Lissa hopped down from the bench, and Gage carefully eased himself down. His head was pounding, and his eyes were dry and sore from fatigue. His jaw ached worse than it had in a long time. But there was a sense of vigor that ran through him at the night's success.

The front doors opened and Torol Stane walked out. His two bodyguards flanked him. The apprehension at the sight of him that Gage had felt at their previous encounter was gone. He had recovered the goods and the man was no threat to him now. He met Torol's eyes easily.

"The master wants to see you." The displeasure in the man's voice was evident.

"I figured he would," Gage said, walking past without hesitation. "Have your apes unload the wagon." He called it back over his shoulder without bothering to turn, though part of him wished to see the man's face redden at the insult. He heard Lissa's quick, light steps as she hurried to catch up to him.

"What an unpleasant looking man." Lissa matched her stride to his as they paced down a long stone corridor.

"Even less pleasant to speak to."

They walked along the stone hallways, turning a few times until they came to the room Gage had visited on his only previous meeting. He knocked on the door and a voice called for him to enter.

Gage opened the heavy oak door and entered the sizeable, well-lit room. It was all dressed stone, with simple yet elegant wooden furniture. The walls were covered in bookcases loaded with all manner of books, scrolls and collections of loose parchments.

There was a large desk against the back wall, and behind sat a small man. He had long, white hair that fell down his back. His snowy beard was braided so it hung down his chest in a single line. His eyes were a soft green, and his white eyebrows rose to an odd peak at the corners.

"Master Waylan." Gage nodded his head to his employer. "This is an old associate of mine." He waved his hand at Lissa and opened his mouth to introduce her, but he was cut off.

"Alissandra DeMar." That Waylan knew her name seemed to shock Lissa. "I have heard of your skills."

"From who?" Lissa said, almost demandingly. In the slums, it was always good to know who was talking about you. But here in the Heights, one didn't ask such things from people like this.

"I have many sources for information, and they keep me well informed of the goings-on of the slums." Waylan steepled his fingers and regarded them intently. "I appreciate your help in recovering my property. And the help of your colleagues. I will see that a generous donation is made to the Fangs." Lissa nodded dumbly at that, obviously stunned at the gesture.

"We are glad to have been of service," Lissa said, remembering her manners. Gage glanced at her. She seemed uneasy at the directness and insight Waylan had displayed. "If there's anything else—"

"Would you like a job, Miss DeMar?"

"What?" Gage and Lissa both asked simultaneously. Gage had a momentary jolt of fear that Waylan meant to replace him. Perhaps recovering the stolen property wasn't enough to earn forgiveness.

"You lost your partner, Faron, in the robbery, Master Gage. I would think you could use a new one?" Gage nodded. Lissa glanced at him, but he could guess nothing of her thoughts.

"How much does it pay?" Lissa asked after a moment.

"Far more than you'll ever earn down in the slums. I am very generous with those who serve me well." He looked at Gage and Gage could do nothing other than nod in agreement. His job was safe at least.

"What would I be doing?" Gage could tell by her tone that she found the offer tempting. He could relate. It was exactly why he had chosen to work for Waylan himself.

"Various things." Waylan said, vaguely. "We can discuss that at a later date. But know this, I will never order you to do something you do not wish to do. That is not how I operate. As for now, you both look like you've had a trying night. Go and rest. We can talk again in a few days."

Gage and Lissa walked back the way they came in silence. As they approached the exit, Gage looked at her.

"What are you going to do?"

Dane woke up to Storr shaking him.

"Damn kid, you were sleeping like the dead. You didn't get up to any trouble last night, did you?"

"No," Dane said, wiping his eyes as he sat up. "Just had trouble sleeping."

He followed Storr into the sitting room, noting that it was already evening. He had slept the whole day.

"How did things go last night?" Dane asked.

"Well enough, well enough." Storr had pulled out his pipe and was packing it with baccin. "We gotta get going, kid. The boss wants to see you."

Dane felt his hackles go up. This seemed sudden. He hadn't expected the gang leader would bother with him until he was ready for real work. He began to worry that someone had found out about his exploits the night before. Storr must have noticed the worry on his face.

"No need to get anxious, kid. The boss doesn't meet with people he intends ill toward. That's what he pays us for. He just wants to see how you're settling in. Nothing to worry about."

Dane forced himself to relax. Nothing to worry about. He repeated it to himself over and over as he followed Storr over to the Smoking Pipe. As they entered, the back door opened, and Lissa exited. She noticed Storr and Dane and headed toward them. She nodded at Storr, then looked at Dane.

"Hey, kid. How's your training going?"

214

"Pretty good."

"That's good." She hesitated, as if about to give some bad news. "Look, I know you were supposed to be my apprentice, but something has come up, and I'm leaving to work with Halfjaw. His boss offered me a job and it's a better one than I'll ever find anywhere else, I would bet."

"You're going private?" Storr's face was stunned. She nodded. "Woah. Bet Grant didn't take that well."

"He did not."

"So, who is gonna train me?" Dane asked. If she wasn't going to be his master, then who would?

"Well, Storr and Tamar are skilled enough to teach you. I'm sure Grant will be fine with you staying with them if you're happy there." She put her hand on his shoulder. "Train hard, kid. Storr says you've got potential. I hope you have the strength to realize it. Good luck." With that, she stepped around them and left the Pipe.

"Wow." Storr whistled through his teeth. "Never thought I'd see her go private. Not that I blame her. A lot more money in it." He looked toward the door standing open at the back of the bar. "Well, no use sitting around wondering about it. Come on, kid."

Storr led him through the door, down a small hallway to another door guarded by the same fat man Dane had seen before. The man nodded at Storr and pushed the door open. Storr prodded Dane forward; evidently, he wasn't coming in with him.

Dane entered the office, looking around at the well-made furniture and fancy decorations. Marcum Grant leaned against the desk at one end of the room, a glass of whiskey in his hand.

"Ah, Dane." The large man came forward, extending his hand. Dane shook it, Grant's red face looming over his own. "Good to see you lad. Training off to a good start?" Dane nodded at that, unsure of how much to elaborate. Grant barely seemed to notice the acknowledgment. "How much thought have you given to your future?"

"Not much, sir. For now, I'm just trying to learn."

"That's wise. The future is a tricky thing. It's smart to focus on the things that are happening now. However, sometimes, it's good to look down the road. Best way to be prepared for what you may find there." Dane nodded to that, though he wasn't sure what to make of it. "I've very recently suffered a loss of personnel that will be difficult to replace."

"Lissa?"

Grant's face twisted briefly. He shook his head, then downed the contents of his glass. He reached for the bottle that sat on his desk and refilled it.

"Yes, that's a big loss. But things change. That is life. And changes must be adapted to, or the world will pass you by. According to Lissa, Storr and Tamar have very good things to say about the early stages of your training. Have you thought about the specialties you might wish to pursue?"

"Not really, sir. I've only just started and haven't even tried all of them yet."

"Keeping your options open. That's smart, too." Grant sat in one of the plush chairs in front of the desk. "Have a seat. I have a proposal for how you might want to proceed in that regard." Dane sat in the chair opposite him.

"After hearing the reports of last night's events. I believe we need a new strategy for training. At least for a few specialized agents. Have you considered practicing Blending?"

"Isn't that very dangerous?"

"It is. But those men that Halfjaw, Lissa, and my men fought last night were all Blenders. Eventually, people are going to begin to see the merits of such men. I wish to get ahead of that curve. And I want to start with you."

Dane considered that. He remembered the rush of coccin from the night before. The feeling of Tamar and Storr pummeling him to no effect in his training session. To combine the two, with real practice, would be something. He thought also of Isar, and the promise the strange man had made to him. About powers from other places. Powers greater than Narcomancy.

But Isar would be gone for Dane didn't know how long. This seemed like a way to grow strong until the day came when or if Isar returned. It was an easy decision, really.

"I think I would like that, sir."

Krayden worked in the back room of his shop by the light of several lanterns. The sound of rain pattering upon the roof was annoying, but there was nothing to be done about it. It was well past midnight, yet he continued to work. He did not need much sleep these days. Besides, he was on the verge of a breakthrough.

He leaned down and inspected the vial that was currently dripping liquid onto a thin sheet-like pan. It was almost clear, with an odd sheen to it. Exactly like the other one had been. He turned back to the other sheet-like pan sitting on the big stone table. This one was practically dry. It looked like slightly tinted glass. It would take some more time for it to be ready to test.

So Krayden set himself about some other small tasks to keep himself from obsessing over the wait. He cleaned the room, though there wasn't much to do in that regard, as he was a fastidiously tidy man. He swept the floor that didn't truly need it and wiped down counters that were already clean enough to eat off of.

Finally, after another hour, he checked the pan again. He tapped it lightly with his gloved finger. It was hard, though not as thick as true glass. He took a tiny hammer and tapped it against the surface. Cracks spiderwebbed out from the impact. He tapped again in the same spot as lightly as he could. A chunk the size of his thumbnail popped free.

He picked the chunk up with a pair of tweezers, holding it up to the light and examining it with a jeweler's eyeglass. The glassy substance was clear, aside from the faint tint. He could barely contain his awe. This might finally be the one. This could be the culmination of his life's work.

Krayden's thoughts were disturbed by a harsh knocking on the outside door of the shop. Irritated, he put the substance down. He debated simply not answering. But it was possible that it was a Narcomancer in need of some clandestine aid. And especially if it were one of the Fangs, Krayden did not want to anger Marcum Grant. It was mainly from Grant's payments that he funded his experiments.

He pushed through the back door and walked to the front door, which was locked and barred. He put his ear to the door.

"Who is it? What do you need?" He called through the thick door. The response he got was muffled. The thick door and the heavy rain made it hard to hear.

"Hells!" Krayden muttered, undoing the lock. He lifted the bar and moved to set it aside. As soon as the bar was lifted, the door was flung open. Three men dressed all in black stormed in. Their faces were covered, as was the rest of their bodies. One of the men reached for Krayden, but the old man was not as defenseless as he appeared.

Krayden jabbed out with the knife he had pulled from the sleeve of his robe. The blade slashed across the palm of the stranger. Normally, such a cut would mean nothing. But this blade was coated with one of the deadliest and fast-acting poisons that Krayden knew of. The man fell back, howling in pain and flailing his injured hands. The screams did not last long.

Krayden scrambled back as the other two men regarded him warily. They glanced at each other and nodded. They pulled out flasks and downed the contents. So, they were Narcomancers. They must have assumed they could take him without needing their powers. Now Krayden's knife would be useless.

They rushed him. Krayden fought as best he could, but they overpowered him easily. In moments, they had him on the ground with a bag over his head. He continued to struggle until one of the men struck him hard on the back of the head, and darkness took him.